LOVE IS PATIENT

PRAIRIE PROMISE BOOK 1

KAY P. DAWSON

CHAPTER 1

The long prairie grass blew in the wind outside the window of the passing stagecoach like waves on the ocean. Kathryn couldn't tear her gaze away from the beauty of the open countryside as they bounced over the rough dirt road. As far as her eyes could see, open fields stretched for miles with only a few trees dotting the landscape between.

She lifted her head to breathe deeply of the fresh, warm air just as the coach hit a bump in the road, knocking her back against her seat. The wheels creaked and groaned beneath her, and she wrapped her arms over her chest as she let herself enjoy the excitement of the new adventure ahead of her.

Promise.

The name of the town in the Dakota Territory had called to her ever since she was a little girl. She'd come to visit her aunt and uncle a few times over the years while growing up, but her father hated everything about small town country life, so they'd never stayed long.

Now, Kathryn was able to make this her home and stay as long as she wanted.

She cringed inwardly at the memory of telling her father about her decision. When her aunt had written to her about a job teaching at the old country school they'd fixed up, Kathryn had known it was meant for her. She'd just completed her teacher's training and had hoped for a position outside the city where she'd grown up.

Kathryn had never felt at home in Boston. She believed her roots were in the country, where her father's family had come from. He'd tried to persuade her away from her "silly notions," as he'd called them, saying that life in the country wasn't for the weak.

Growing up, her father had moved many times while his family tried to survive life on the frontier. He said they'd had nothing, and at times had barely managed to find enough food to live. That's why he'd left as soon as he could to make a life for himself away from the poverty he'd known. He'd worked hard to become a lawyer so he could live in the city where his own family would never have to know the hardships he'd grown up with.

So, when she'd told him she was moving out west, to the Dakota Territory where his brother lived, he'd been angry. He'd spent days trying to talk her out of it but had finally relented enough to say he would support her decision. Then added, he'd welcome her back home once she came to her senses and realized life on the frontier wasn't as romantic as she was imagining.

"We're just outside of Promise now, Miss. If you look out the window on your right-hand side, you'll see that schoolhouse you'll be teaching at." The driver called down to her, startling her from her thoughts.

Before they'd left Brookings this morning, she'd been so excited, so she'd eagerly told the kind older man everything about what she was coming out here to do. He'd said he'd let her know as soon as they were close enough for her to see the schoolhouse.

She leaned against the side of the coach once more, not even caring about the jarring her body was taking with every bump. The small building she could see in the distance had her heart racing with joy. The few times she'd visited Promise as a child, she'd never paid much attention to the school outside of town.

It sat in the middle of a field, with just a few trees nearby, painted the same color as the barn she could see up the road. Her aunt had told her all about how the community had come together to bring the old schoolhouse back into working order, fixing it up and painting it with leftover red paint some of the farmers in the area had donated.

And now, this was going to be her schoolhouse. The small tower over the door housed a bell that she could already picture herself ringing to announce the start and end of the school day. The sound would alert the families that the children were on their way home so they would know to watch for them.

Off to the side, she could see the small cabin where she would be staying, nestled among the trees on the property. She smiled as she imagined how mortified her father would be right now if he was looking at the same scene out the window as she was.

But in her eyes, it all looked perfect. It was

everything she'd dreamed about since the first time she'd come to visit her aunt and uncle so many years ago.

The wheels bounced loudly over the wooden bridge leading into the town. Everything looked the same from her last visit here, except for a few new buildings, and it seemed like there were more people who came out to wave at the passing stagecoach.

With a cloud of dust wrapping around them, they lurched to a stop in front of her aunt's boardinghouse where passengers would get to rest a bit before continuing on their journey. However, Kathryn was the only one arriving today, and as the driver opened the door and offered his hand, she stepped onto the wooden walkway. Before she even had time to take in the view around her, she was grabbed into a tight embrace.

"Kathryn! Oh, my goodness child, you look exactly the same as you did the last time I saw you. What has it been? It must be over eight years ago by now. You were just a young girl then."

She laughed and hugged her beloved aunt back tightly. "I was almost thirteen and I remember being so excited to be here, but my father complained about everything, so it didn't make it much fun."

Her aunt pulled back, still holding onto her arms as she looked her up and down. "Well, now you're here on your own and you can have the chance to enjoy life in the country. I know you're going to love it here. There are so many young women around your age to be friends with, and the school we've fixed up will just be a wonderful place for your first teaching job."

"Lucy, step back and let the poor girl have a chance to catch her breath." Her uncle Martin walked over and helped the driver lift her trunk down. He smiled warmly at her, then came over to give her a hug. Her heart tugged slightly at how much he looked like her father. "It's good to see you, Kathryn. Once your aunt here is finished fussing over you, we've got a nice warm meal ready for you inside."

Her aunt looped her arm into hers to lead her up the boardinghouse steps while her uncle and the driver followed, talking about the weather and the trip here from Brookings.

"We'll let you get cleaned up and rested here tonight, then tomorrow we'll run you out to the Hammond farm to meet the owners of the property the school sits on. Mrs. Hammond has spent the past few days scrubbing the cabin you'll be living in from top to bottom, making it all ready for you. And we'll let you see inside the school you'll be teaching in."

Kathryn wasn't sure it was possible for anyone to be any more excited than she was, but her aunt Lucy was certainly coming close. Since they'd never had children of their own, Kathryn figured this was her chance to dote on someone, even if she was a grown woman.

Before she was pulled inside the door, Kathryn quickly let her eyes move around the town she would now call home. The mercantile across the street stood proudly in the center, and the church behind it sat with the door open and inviting. A few townsfolk mingled around, shouting greetings to passing wagons.

In her heart, Kathryn knew this was the place she was meant to be. And she couldn't wait to prove it to her father, herself, and anyone else who might doubt it.

CHAPTER 2

*C*olt reached up and pushed his hat back to wipe at the sweat on his forehead. The heat from the sun was already scorching and it wasn't even midday. But he was almost finished putting in the last of his crop for this year, so he was determined to keep going, even if he did fall from heat exhaustion. The past few years had been difficult for the farmers in the area, so he was hopeful this year he'd have a good crop. The sooner it was in the ground, the better chance he had.

His gaze moved around the field he stood in, with the dust swirling up around his face from the slight breeze that blew over the land. The leather of the harness holding the horses to the plow squeaked with the movement of the animals as they waited for the signal to start moving again. But otherwise there was blessed silence.

He'd grown up on this land, and no matter how many times he looked at it, pride swelled up inside him. His parents had been the first settlers in the area and had been a driving force when creating the town of Promise all those years ago. Even though there had been times when it would have been easier to sell everything and move somewhere with better opportunities, instead of struggling to bring in enough to feed his family, he knew he could never leave.

This land was in his blood and he was determined his own children would know the same sense of pride he did.

Some days, he wished he could have been more like his younger brother, Luke, who'd joined the cavalry as soon as he'd been old enough so he could see more of the country. He'd always been more of an adventurous type than Colt and had never really seemed to enjoy farming anyway.

They'd both worked alongside their father from the time they were old enough to walk, tending to the chores and helping with the crops, but it had always been obvious Colt was more interested in taking over the farm. After their father had passed away when Colt was just seventeen, he'd stepped up and carried on supporting the family the best he could.

A wagon coming up the road toward the house caught his eye and he cursed under his breath. He didn't have time to be making small talk with the new schoolteacher in town, but his mother had given him a stern lecture this morning that he was to be present and cleaned up when she arrived.

Now he was going to have to face them both wearing clothes covered in dirt and sweat. He knew his face was likely the same color as the land he stood on, so any chances of making a good first impression were gone now.

Not that he really cared much anyway. He'd known the Reeves in town for many years, and they were wonderful people, so he was sure their niece was a nice enough woman. But she came from the city, so he knew she would hate it out here from the start.

Oh, she'd be excited and think it was a grand adventure in the beginning, just like his wife, Arlene, had when she first came to live here. But within a few months of being here and seeing the reality of life on the frontier, she would quickly realize it wasn't as romantic as she'd imagined.

He just hoped the children of Promise didn't get too attached to her before she ran back home.

He flicked the reins to get the horses moving, cringing as he imagined the scolding he was going to get from his mother once the guests were gone. He was a grown man, but she wasn't afraid to still put her foot down now and again to remind him of how she'd raised him to know better.

He knew, though, that even if he ran to the house, he wasn't going to make it there before them. So any chance of cleaning himself up to be presentable was gone.

As soon as he led the horses around the corner of the barn into the yard, he could feel his mother's disapproving glare. He quickly unhitched them and pretended he wasn't intimidated at all by the looks he was getting from the people standing just beside the wagon.

He walked toward them with a wide grin on his face, acting like he was dressed in his finest and wasn't covered from head to toe in grime. His eyes immediately fell on the woman who had to be the new teacher, and his step faltered slightly. His chest gave a tug as he realized he'd never antici-pated that she would be so beautiful.

She was smiling back at him and didn't seem to be in the least bit disgusted that he hadn't cleaned up to meet her.

"Miss Reeves, this is my son, Mr. Colt Hammond. I apologize for his lack of manners, but obviously he forgot he'd be showing you around the place today." His mother shot him a disap-proving stare before continuing with the introduc-tions. "And, Colt, this is Miss Kathryn Reeves, the new teacher at the school."

He smiled sheepishly at the woman who'd already put her hand out for him to take. He slowly removed his tattered and worn work gloves, wondering if it would be rude to wipe his hands on his dirty pants before offering his hand. "I'm sorry, Miss, but you likely don't want me to take your hand. I'm afraid my gloves don't do much for keeping the dirt out, and I'd hate to get any on you."

She laughed, the sound sending warm shivers through his body. "Don't be silly. I'm not scared of a little dirt." She reached out and took his hand, shaking it as she smiled up at him. "It's nice to meet you, Mr. Hammond. I think I might remember seeing you once or twice on my visits to town when I was a girl, but I doubt you'd remember me. I can't wait to see the schoolhouse, and the little cabin I'll be staying in."

He swallowed and tried to catch up to what she was saying. But from the moment she'd taken his hand, without any concern about the sweat and grime, he'd been at a loss for words. The excitement she was feeling was palpable, and for a moment he truly did feel guilty for not making sure he'd been cleaned up.

The truth was, he knew deep down he'd done it on purpose. He knew this woman wasn't going to be any different than his wife had been, so he hadn't wanted to give her any false pretenses about what she could expect from living out here.

But she'd surprised him by not seeming to be affected at all. Colt knew it wouldn't last, though. His eyes moved over her silky dress that would never stand up to life out here. It was clear she'd grown up pampered and never wanting for anything, so he would give her until the first snowfall, if she even lasted that long.

"It's nice to meet you too, Miss Reeves. I'll just go in and get changed so I can take you out to the schoolhouse. Hopefully, you won't be too disappointed in your living quarters."

He almost laughed to himself as he walked away, knowing full well she was going to be mortified when she saw the little shack set back from the school that she'd be living in. It was the original cabin used by the teachers, including his old teacher Miss Fernly.

There wasn't much in the little cabin, although his mother had fixed it up quite a bit when she'd briefly lived in it after he'd been married. So, he knew it was perfectly adequate.

He just didn't believe it would be enough for a city girl to live in, so he was prepared for the fit of hysterics—and not the laughing kind—he was most likely about to witness.

Hopefully, it wouldn't take long because he had a field to get back to work in and coddling a fainting city girl wasn't in his plans for today.

CHAPTER 3

"This is perfect! It's just how I pictured it would be." Kathryn slowly turned, letting her eyes take it all in. The chalkboards were scratched and faded, not at all like the pristine ones she'd had in her own school in Boston, but she could imagine the lessons that had been shared on them.

The desks were made by hand, but she could tell they were sturdy and would give the students somewhere comfortable to spend their days. Her fingers reached down to open one of the brand-new readers sitting on her own desk, and she inhaled deeply as the scent of the fresh paper reached her nose.

"It's likely a great deal smaller than what

you're used to, but this little schoolhouse has taught many children through the years. Well, until it had to be closed down a few years ago when the new private school was built in town. I'm afraid we never imagined it would be reopened, so it had started to fall into a bit of disrepair."

Kathryn smiled over at Mrs. Winnie Hammond, the kind older woman who was still standing near the doorway with her arms around the two shy children on either side of her.

When she'd been introduced to Mr. Hammond's twin children, Delia and Owen, they'd both been polite but reserved in their greetings. She sensed that Delia was desperately fighting the urge to talk to her, but for some reason her brother was making sure she kept her distance.

"I hear you two were a big help in getting this schoolhouse back into shape. I can't thank you enough for all your hard work. You both did a great job." She offered the children a smile, hoping they would open up to her a bit more.

Delia smiled shyly and nodded her head. "I helped wash the windows and the floors. And I helped paint the outside too, but just the bottom of the walls where I could reach."

"Well, it looks perfect. This is just about the nicest schoolhouse I've ever seen."

Owen pulled his eyebrows together suspiciously. "I thought you grew up in the big city. I don't believe you. Your schools would have been a lot fancier than this one."

Mr. Hammond stood off to the side, leaning back against a desk with his arms crossed over his chest. He shook his head at his son, shooting him an angry look. "Owen! Remember your manners."

The young boy quickly looked down at his shoes. "I'm sorry, Miss."

"No, Owen, you're right. The school I went to in Boston was quite a bit fancier than this, but I have to tell you a secret." He slowly lifted his gaze to hers. She offered him a smile as she scrunched up her nose. "It was fancy, but it smelled really bad inside. And, there were hardly any windows to look outside, so it was always dark. It really wasn't a very nice place to be. That's why I say this is the nicest school I've ever seen. It truly is." She went over by the window closest to her and waved her hand toward it. "See that? It's so nice to be able to see outside, and enjoy feeling the sunshine on our skin, even when we're inside learning. You don't know how lucky you are to have grown up where you can see for miles." She took a deep breath in and closed her eyes for a few moments. "And everything smells so fresh."

Delia's eyes were wide as she listened. "What did it smell like in your school?"

Kathryn laughed as she walked over by the children and crouched down in front of them to whisper her answer. "Well, don't ever tell anyone I told you this, but in my school it always smelled like dirty feet and horse manure."

Owen's face broke out in a smile before he quickly tried to hide it. But Delia couldn't. She brought her hand up to her mouth and giggled.

"That would have been awful!"

Kathryn nodded seriously. "It was. And that's why I'm so glad it doesn't smell like that in here." She gave a small shudder as she winked at Delia.

She stood back up and faced Mr. Hammond. As soon as her eyes met his, the smile dropped from her face. She couldn't tell if he was angry with her or how he was feeling, but something in his stance told her he wasn't happy.

"You've seen the schoolhouse, so let's get to the cabin where you'll be staying. I don't have all day to be showing everyone around. I have a field to finish planting." He pushed himself past her toward the door. Kathryn looked nervously toward Mrs. Hammond who was scowling at her son's retreating back.

Thankfully, her aunt had come with them too, and now she came over to put her arm around Kathryn's shoulder as they followed him out the door, leaning in close to whisper in her ear, "Don't worry about Colt Hammond, dear. He's a bit rough around the edges sometimes."

Mrs. Hammond came behind them with the children in tow and as they walked through the tall grass toward the cabin, Kathryn's cheeks burned as she wondered what she'd done to make him angry with her.

But she couldn't spend too much time worrying, because as they walked, the gentle breeze kissed her cheeks and took away any doubts that had started to creep in.

This was where she was meant to be. She could feel it in the air around her and with every step she took, her heart swelled even more with joy. She'd never felt like this walking in the city. The ground crunched under her boots and she let her hands trail over the top of the long, feathery grasses along the path. Above them, birds sang from the trees standing behind the small cabin.

"There's a well right there with a pump for your water, and just behind the trees there's a small creek that runs through the property you can use too if you want." Kathryn looked over to the rickety-looking pump that Mr. Hammond was pointing to as they stopped in front of the cabin. He turned slightly and pointed to a small building off on its own. "And that's your outhouse. It's not much, but it keeps the wild animals out. You'll want to use a lantern after dark. The students will use it during the day too."

She hoped the shock on her face wasn't too evident because she could tell that he was watching closely for her reaction. For some reason, she'd never really thought about the facilities she'd be using out here and the thought of using a rundown outhouse in the middle of nowhere was more unnerving than she cared to admit.

Mrs. Hammond came up beside her and put her hand on her arm. "Oh, he makes it sound like it's so primitive. For goodness sake, Colt." His mother shook her head in disgust at her son before smiling back at Kathryn. "There's a chamber pot inside the cabin you can use after dark."

Kathryn wasn't sure how much better a

chamber pot would be which she'd have to carry out to empty, but she would never let the broody man see her concern.

And she wasn't about to let it spoil her excitement about everything else. She was sure she'd get used to the more primitive aspects of life on the prairies over time.

When she walked through the door into her new home, which was nothing more than one room with a curtain blocking off a bed in the back, she had one more wave of doubt hit her.

Could she really do this?

For some reason, the smug look on Mr. Hammond's face, telling her he knew full well she was a city girl who would never survive out here on her own, made any doubts quickly fall away.

One thing Mr. Colt Hammond was about to learn about her was that she would never back down from a challenge. This had been her dream all her life, and she was more determined than ever to follow it through.

Even if she did have to brave a crumbling down outhouse full of spiders in the dark.

CHAPTER 4

"Well, I have to say she's not quite what I expected. Not really sure what I was thinking, but I guess since she's Lucy Reeves's niece I was expecting someone a little smaller. And plumper, maybe."

Colt laughed as his friend Caleb's wife slapped him hard on the arm. "Caleb Bailey. Can't you think before you speak out loud? What if she heard you!"

Fae Bailey gave her husband a stern look, then turned to make sure Colt knew she didn't appreciate him encouraging her husband's behavior.

When Fae had arrived in Promise, she'd quickly made her mark on the small town. She'd come from New York, where she'd been raised in an orphanage built on the principle of equal opportunities for education. Fae had agreed to come here and marry Caleb, without ever having met him, with the knowledge she also wanted to help all the children in the area receive an education.

Of course, she'd hoped to find love with her husband too, which Colt was still surprised had worked out as it had. Especially knowing his friend's aversion to ever settling down.

Now, the couple were head over heels in love and running the mercantile in town. It was so out of character with what he'd imagined Caleb ever doing, but for some reason, they'd both settled into married life and seemed happier than any couple Colt had ever known.

A hard lump formed in his stomach at the thought, and he clenched his jaw tight as he pushed his feelings away. Now wasn't the time to start thinking about his wife, or how easily he'd been duped into believing they were happily married at one time too.

"I think she seems perfect, and I know the kids in town are going to love her. Look how taken Delia already is with her." Fae smiled warmly toward the people they were discussing.

Colt's eyes followed Fae's to where his daughter

was enthusiastically telling a story to Miss Reeves with her arms flapping and head nodding excitedly. They were beside a table filled with pitchers of lemonade and every kind of food imaginable set in the center of town for the new teacher's welcome party. It seemed like most of the townsfolk had shown up to have a chance to meet her. Well, everyone except for the Pembrookes who ran the private school, and the few "wealthier" families in the area who believed this new public school would be a blemish to their community.

On this sunny afternoon, the entire ground between the church and the boardinghouse was filled with people as they milled around between the tables, enjoying the chance to have this community get-together after church. Kids ran around, filled with excitement knowing tomorrow would be their first day of school.

Some of them had never had the chance to have any kind of education, so this was an opportunity he knew was desperately needed in this town. When the private school had been opened a few years ago, it was hard to keep the old school going. The Pembrookes had made sure it was clear the education would never be as good as what could be offered by the new Pembrooke School. The children who went to school there would have the best opportunities for education which would lead them into highly respectable and advantageous careers. It would open more doors for a better life than the small country schoolhouse ever could.

Colt knew of families who'd almost gone completely broke trying to pay for the best schooling for their children. So many wanted their children to have better lives than what they'd had, and desperation had led a few of them to lose everything. There had been several families who even had to move away to start over somewhere else. But people had falsely believed this new private school was the best thing for the community, until it was too late to realize how much it was actually hurting the small town.

Keeping the old public school going out on the Hammond property had been hard, and as enrolment declined due to the initial excitement of the private school, finding teachers willing to work for what the community could offer to pay was difficult. There weren't many women wanting to come out to the middle of the prairies, in a small town without much to offer. By the time many of the families realized they couldn't continue paying the fees for the private school, it was too late. The public school had to be closed and no one seemed to know how to get it going again.

Until Fae arrived, and set things in motion to bring it back. And, thanks to an inheritance from his father, Caleb had made sure the school could afford everything it needed.

Colt continued to watch the new schoolteacher and could only imagine what the child was talking about. He inwardly cringed, hoping it wasn't anything too farfetched. His daughter had a vivid imagination and tended to add a little extra excitement to her stories.

But Miss Reeves was completely enthralled as she crouched down to make sure she could hear every detail. He let his gaze stay on the woman while he vaguely heard Fae talking about how nice the new teacher had seemed when they met earlier.

As she bent down and leaned in to listen to Delia, he noticed the skirt she wore. It wasn't silk, like the dress she'd been wearing when she arrived yesterday, but it was still a much nicer fabric than most of the women wore around here. He wondered how long it would hold up to being washed with the harsh soaps and cold creek water available to her now.

"She's not going to last a month out here. The warm early summer we're having is nice, but once the full heat hits, she won't be able to stand it. And there's no way she'll ever be able to endure the cold of our winters."

Fae gasped and turned back to glare at Colt. "You don't know anything about her. How are you so sure she won't be able to handle being here? I'm sure you all thought the same thing about me when I arrived. Are you saying you don't think I'll be able to survive the winter out here either? After all, I'm just a city girl from back east too."

Colt ignored the look on Caleb's face who was struggling not to laugh while his wife scolded his best friend.

"No, I have no doubt you'll be just fine, Fae. You grew up in an orphanage, so you understand about struggles and hardships. What difficulties did Miss Reeves have growing up? From what I've heard, she was raised in a wealthy family and most likely never had to do anything for herself. It's a completely different world out here than it is where she comes from. That's all I'm saying."

But Fae was already too riled up to listen to him. She shook her head and crossed her arms over her chest. "Well, I think you're being completely unfair and judging her before you've even given her a chance. I see a woman who's excited for something new. She's strong enough to walk away from the so-called *pampered* life you say she had back home to head west, and *completely on her own*, to start a new life. So, you better just mind your manners and make her feel welcome."

Colt's mouth hung open as he watched Fae walk over to talk to Miss Reeves. Another young woman from town, Mercy Brown, joined the women and he could see Fae introducing them. He noticed Kathryn take Delia's hand, to make sure the child still felt included, and his chest clenched at the image.

His friend whistled softly beside him. "Whoa. I'm sure glad it's you who riled her up this time and not me."

"I didn't mean to upset her. I mean, I have complete confidence that Fae will have no trouble at all surviving out here. She's just different than Miss Reeves is."

Caleb brought his brows together and turned to look at him. "How do you know that? You barely know her. All you know is what you think she grew up with."

Colt pretended to ignore Caleb.

"And, you can't compare everyone to how Arlene was."

Anger rose inside Colt as he fought the sudden urge to knock his friend out. "Don't bring her up. I'm not comparing anyone to her."

Caleb just shrugged, ignoring the fact he was walking on thin ice.

"Just because Arlene was a city girl, and quickly proved she wasn't cut out for the more primitive life out here, doesn't mean every woman who comes here is the same."

Colt kept his teeth clenched tightly and bit his tongue from saying anything. Just because Caleb was now a happily married man, he didn't need to act like he was suddenly an expert on everything that had to do with women.

Colt was the one who had wasted his time, and a piece of his heart, with a woman who couldn't handle the frontier life. And he recognized it when he saw another woman just like her.

Miss Kathryn Reeves wouldn't be here come the winter.

He guaranteed it.

CHAPTER 5

"Well, I don't remember the last time so many people showed up for church. Reverend Moore was beside himself with excitement. The church was overflowing, thanks to all the folks who wanted the chance to mingle and meet the new schoolteacher after." Mrs. Hammond turned around to smile at Kathryn.

Just then, the wagon bounced, making her wince slightly as her back banged against the wooden side. She rode in the back with the children, while Mrs. Hammond and her son were up front. Kathryn worried the rickety seat along the side for them to sit on would fall apart with one more bump.

Delia was sitting right beside her, almost as

though she was afraid to let Kathryn out of her sight. But Owen still hadn't seemed to warm up to her at all. He sat facing away from her, leaning his chin on his arms that rested along the wagon's edge, his eyes watching the land as they bounced along the dirt road.

"It was nice to meet everyone. I hope I can remember everyone's name the next time I see them. Especially all the children I met. I hope they're all still as excited tomorrow as they seemed today."

Mrs. Hammond nodded and turned back to face forward beside her son. "Oh, it will take you some time to remember all the names. And every one of the children you met today was overcome with excitement for the chance to go to school tomorrow. You're going to be busy, so we'll let you have a chance to get settled in a bit, then you can come up to the house for supper. I have no doubt you'll feel tired after all the traveling and excitement of the past few days."

Kathryn smiled warmly at the back of her head. Her flowery bonnet covered her head, but Kathryn could picture the tight bun her hair would be pulled into beneath it.

Tonight would be her first night out in the

small cabin next to the school, and though she was reluctant to admit it, she was nervous about being all alone out there.

All her life, she'd had her family and servants around her, but now she'd be completely on her own. She knew the Hammonds were just across the field, but in the dark, she was sure it would seem like they were miles away.

She gently shook her head, trying to get rid of the small fears that were threatening. Her aunt and uncle had let her stay with them last night, and she'd felt safe and comfortable. They'd tried to convince her to stay there, even if it was just for a little bit longer until she had a chance to settle into her new role.

Her gaze moved to the back of Colt's large brimmed hat as he drove the team of horses out of town. She swallowed hard as she remembered the smug look he'd had on his face when her aunt had tried to convince her to stay one more time as they were packing her few belongings into the wagon. For some reason, seeing the expression on his face had made Kathryn even more determined, when otherwise, she was sure she might have taken her aunt up on the offer.

Now, there was no turning back without

admitting to Colt Hammond, and everyone else, that she wasn't cut out for living here on her own.

She smiled down at the little girl who was now resting up against her and put her arm around her to pull her in close. Kathryn welcomed the warmth of the small body bouncing into her with every movement of the wagon. It was almost like she could take some courage from the fact that this child believed in her.

Her eyes went across to the boy with his back to her. She wasn't sure why he seemed so determined not to let himself get close, but she hoped over time he would accept her. She looked past him to the miles of open fields beyond the wagon. Some of them had just been worked, but she could already see sprouts of green popping through the dirt in the ones planted earlier. It was something she'd never been able to see in the city—the new ground having been plowed and prepared to allow the seed and new life to burst through.

It excited her as she thought back to the times she'd visited her aunt as a child. She'd often secretly walked outside of the town to sit under a tree and close her eyes, listening to the sounds around her and breathing in the fresh air. The growing crops rustling in the breeze had soothed her, and even as a young girl, she truly had believed her heart belonged here.

She swallowed hard as she tried to remind herself of those feelings, instead of the worry and doubt that had started to creep in. The knowledge that she would be able to watch this land turn green, then yellow, and brown as it filled with the food of the land, gave her a new sense of excitement.

She knew she could do this, even if the man in the seat in front of her seemed to believe otherwise.

And as they bounced up alongside the cabin nestled back among the trees, she repeated those words over and over in her head. She reminded herself how excited she was for this chance, and how beautiful this new little home of hers was.

With a sudden jolt, she realized, this *was* all hers. She'd never had a home to call her own before, and while this was nowhere near as glamorous or sturdy as the house she'd grown up in, her eyes almost filled with tears at the joy she felt looking at the wooden walls. This was where she was starting her new life, and she was determined it would be everything that little girl under the tree had always dreamed it would be.

"I'm so excited for you to be living here. I can come over and visit all the time. When I'm not in school, I mean." Delia jumped up and clapped her hands together as Kathryn stood, holding onto the back of the seat in front for balance.

"Now, Delia, remember what we told you. Miss Reeves isn't to be bothered, and that means you aren't to be coming down here uninvited. She's your teacher, so you will see her plenty enough during school hours."

Kathryn smiled down at the little girl's suddenly shy and embarrassed face. "It's all right, Mrs. Hammond. I'm sure I would welcome a visit from both Delia and Owen any time they want. I'll need someone to help me with some of the chores around here that only a man can do, so I hope you don't mind helping me out, Owen."

She hoped the young boy would feel a sense of pride at being asked to help her, giving him a reason to trust her. But he just shrugged and nodded his head as he hopped down from the wagon. "I can help, I guess. But I've got my own chores to do, and now I'm likely going to have homework too." His voice didn't sound impressed at that prospect.

"Owen." His father shot him a disapproving look.

"Don't you worry, dear. Between Owen and Colt, they'll make sure you have everything done around here that you need. And if you ever need anything, all you have to do is come up to the house and ask." Mrs. Hammond smoothed over the awkward moment and walked around to the back of the wagon after her son had helped her down. Kathryn's heart did a leap as she realized he was now standing there at the open back waiting to help her too.

She'd managed to climb into the wagon with the help of her uncle when they'd left, and she hadn't quite thought it through how she would get down. And, she wasn't entirely sure why it both-ered her so much that she'd now have to rely on this man's help.

She pushed away the sudden thought that she'd have to take his hand, and for some reason, it made her nervous. It wasn't like she'd never had a man help her in or out of a carriage before, so she couldn't quite figure out what was wrong with her.

He grabbed Delia with both hands around the waist and lifted her high into the air, making the child squeal with delight. "Daddy, don't drop me!"

He laughed as he spun around and set her on the ground beside him. "I'd never drop you. You know that."

Now, he lifted his eyes and met Kathryn's. She couldn't be sure, but she almost thought she could see a glimmer of mischief in the dark eyes staring back at her. For a man who'd seemed terribly grumpy since she'd met him, she knew she had to be imagining it.

But when she walked to the back of the wagon and bent down to let him take her hand, he grabbed her around the waist as quickly as he'd done his daughter and spun her around to the ground before she'd even had a chance to scream.

"Colt Hammond. That is no way to be treating our guest and a lady." Mrs. Hammond came over and slapped Colt hard on the arm before reaching out to wind her arm into Kathryn's. "I apologize for my son's manners. Honestly, I don't know what goes on in his head sometimes. Let's get your things inside your cabin and you can have a chance to freshen up before supper."

Kathryn let the older woman lead her toward the door, her heart still beating twice as fast as it should be. While she'd been startled at being grabbed so quickly, she knew that wasn't the only thing that had gotten her ruffled.

As she quickly glanced back over her shoulder and saw the man standing there grinning beside his children, she knew she'd have to be careful around him.

She was here to teach and start a life without depending on anyone but herself, in a place she'd always dreamed of living.

Not to get her legs swept out from beneath her by the likes of Colt Hammond.

CHAPTER 6

She walked up the center aisle, running her fingers along the handmade desks where the slates sat waiting for the students to practice their lessons. The school had been well stocked, thanks to the donation from Caleb Bailey at the mercantile. It wasn't anywhere near as grand as what she'd had in her school back home, but there was something about this small one room schoolhouse that gave her excited chills.

Maybe it was the anticipation over what lay ahead for her, and how she was now responsible for teaching these children. If not for her coming out here to teach, maybe some of them would never receive any kind of education.

She walked outside and looked across the open

fields, taking a deep breath of the fresh air while the gentle breeze tugged strands of hair loose from her combs. She'd been up before the sun today, even though she'd barely slept a wink last night.

After having a delicious supper of roast beef, potatoes, and fresh apple pie, Mr. Hammond and the children had walked her back to her cabin. Since it was still early summer, the sky had been lit up with the bright orange and purple of a prairie sunset. She'd told them she could manage getting back home on her own, but Mrs. Hammond had insisted her son escort her.

He'd been pleasant enough during the meal and had been a perfect gentleman on the walk to the cabin. But she sensed that he didn't really like her very much, and that bothered her.

Of course, she hadn't had much time to think about it after they'd left, and she'd been by herself as the skies turned dark. She had so much to learn about managing out here on her own. For one thing, she needed to remember to get water from the well and have some in the basin to wash with in the morning so it wouldn't be freezing cold.

So many things were different out here, and what she'd always taken for granted would no longer be done for her.

As she'd climbed into her warm bed last night, the dark had seemed to close in on her and she hadn't wanted to shut her lantern off. A window had been left open against the heat of the day, and in the distance, she'd heard howling noises that had terrified her. It sounded like an entire army of large animals intent on killing anyone who dared to go near them. At one point, she was sure they were right under her window, and she'd quickly run over to close it against the possible intruders.

She wasn't even sure she wanted to ask anyone what they were. All she knew was that she would never be stepping foot outside in the dark by herself.

By the time exhaustion had finally taken over, the first rays of sun were already coming through the window. Thankfully, the excitement of her first day of teaching had kept her from falling asleep standing up so far. But it was going to be a long day.

She reached up and pulled the rope to set the bell ringing. Her heart jumped as the sound belted out across the open land. She knew there would already be children walking from their homes, and she hoped they were as excited to hear the bell as she was. After giving it a few good tugs to make sure it had been heard far and wide, she stood waiting at the top of the steps to meet her first students.

"Good morning, Miss Reeves! I'm so excited!"

She turned her head slightly to see Delia and Owen coming along the path that led up to their house. The girl was excitedly running, struggling to hold onto her lunch pail and book she was holding. She'd been so excited yesterday for homework, she'd asked to take one home even though Kathryn knew she wouldn't be able to read it.

Owen, on the other hand, was walking as slowly as his legs would allow, kicking at a stone ahead of him. He was obviously not as thrilled about the first day of school as his sister.

"You can go on in and sit at your desk up front, Delia. Owen, if you want to take one next to her, you can."

He gave a little shrug and followed his excited sister inside. Kathryn wished she could take the child into her arms for a hug, but she knew he would never allow it. She just hoped that someday she could get through to him and earn his trust. Her aunt had let her know that Mr. Hammond and his wife were estranged, so she knew the children had both been through a lot with their mother

LOVE IS PATIENT

leaving them. She was prepared to give the boy both the time and space he needed to heal.

"Hello, Miss Reeves!" A little girl raced up the path from one of the neighboring farms. "I was up before the sun this morning, and my pa said it was too early, but I got ready anyway. I had all my chores done before breakfast and even had some time to play with my kittens. My ma was cross with me because she said I was going to get my nice dress all dusty before my first day of school."

Kathryn laughed at the joyful exuberance of the small blonde-haired girl. "Well, I think you look lovely, Hazel."

She remembered meeting the child yesterday when she'd been running around with Delia. Normally, the children in the community only got to see their friends at church and the occasional gathering put on in town. Going to school was going to be so much fun, giving them the chance to be together every day.

Hazel ran inside with a huge grin on her face, just as more children showed up. Kathryn greeted them all, and there were only a few whose names she couldn't remember. She'd met so many people yesterday she was surprised she'd managed to keep any of them straight.

43

When she finally went inside, she stopped at the back of the classroom and took a deep breath. Her cheeks hurt from the smile that had been in place since she'd woken up this morning, and as she looked around at the excited faces in front of her, she couldn't imagine ever wanting to be anywhere else. The chatter and laughter filled the room. She knew she needed to get control and set the rules for the classroom, but for this brief moment, she just wanted to take it all in. This was what she'd been dreaming of doing since she was a little girl, when she'd been sitting in her own classroom and listening to her teacher share her knowledge with all of them.

Yes, her classroom even all those years ago had been much more modern, but what she had here was just about close to perfect in her mind.

And as she walked to the front of the room, clapping her hands for attention, she realized being here during the day might be just enough to forget how scared she was alone in her cabin in the dark.

CHAPTER 7

"*How* ow is the plowing going on the land behind your west field? Is your neighbor still trying to cause you problems?"

Colt threw another bag of feed into the back of his wagon before turning to face Mr. King, or Old Tom as everyone around town called him, who owned the feed mill. The old man wasn't much help with any heavy lifting anymore, but he refused to sell the mill, saying he'd die of boredom if he wasn't there every day to visit with the farmers who came in. He had one man working for him who did most of the work, while Old Tom spent his days gossiping with the customers.

"I'm not paying any attention to Constantine Brown. He just wants a fight. I've got the surveyor's reports and I know where my land ends. I'm nowhere near his land."

Constantine Brown had applied to homestead the land bordering Colt's two years ago and had been a thorn in his side ever since. He argued that the land Colt was clearing for a new field was on his property, even though he'd been shown the surveyor reports numerous times. He was the type of man who wanted an argument about everything.

Old Tom shook his head. "I'll never know how that poor woman puts up with a husband like him. I'm sure if he wasn't the nephew of Mrs. Pembrooke, there isn't a person in this town who'd have anything nice to say about the man."

"You're right about that. As far as I'm concerned, Mrs. Brown is a saint because no other woman would have married him."

Colt turned and nodded a greeting as the blacksmith, Layne Perkins, walked up behind them and joined the conversation. His shop was right next door to the feed mill, so he would often come over to say hello when he saw Colt there. He'd been good friends with Colt's brother growing up, and they'd known each other since they were children.

"Well, I'm sure the poor woman didn't have any idea of what she was getting into when she agreed to come here and marry him. I never saw the advertisement he put out for a bride, but I have serious doubts he was honest in it. By the time Mrs. Brown arrived here, and got to know the man he was, it was likely too late for her to change her mind. And now the poor soul is expecting his child, who I'm sure the man won't treat any better."

As though talking about him was enough to make him appear, Brown's wagon bounced loudly over the small bridge into town in a large cloud of dust. Colt groaned to himself as the wagon turned toward the feed mill.

Mrs. Brown sat stiffly in the seat beside him, and as they stopped next to his wagon, she smiled down at Colt. He held his hand up to help her down while her husband hopped down and walked straight up onto the steps of the mill.

"Thank you, Mr. Hammond. I need to run these eggs over to the mercantile. I always try to be here first thing in the morning, but today I guess time got away from me. I was cleaning out the stalls in the barn where one of our horses had a new foal last night."

Colt offered her a smile, clenching his teeth

47

together in anger at the fatigue he could see reflected in her eyes. He knew without a doubt she'd have been cleaning those stalls out on her own, even with her newly expanding waistline which would make the chore more difficult.

"Hammond, you make sure you don't get any closer to that tree line with your plow. You have more than enough land cleared for your crops. Don't see why you need to keep pushing onto my land."

Colt took a deep breath and turned to grab the last bag of feed off the dock that ran around the building. He threw it into the back of his wagon, continuing to ignore the man who was pushing him for a fight.

"If you stop by tomorrow, I'll have that axe finished for you." Layne came over to help him push the back of the wagon closed. Colt nodded, gladly accepting the change in topic.

By now, the town had become busier with the end of the school day. The parents who came in to pick up the kids still attending the Pembrooke School kicked dust up on their way past. Colt noticed there were a few children coming the other way, carrying books and skipping across the bridge coming from the schoolhouse on his property. He could see the pure happiness on their faces as they raced home to tell their parents about their first day of school.

"Must say, that new schoolteacher you got living out there with you sure isn't hard to look at. Lucky for you, you aren't saddled with a nagging wife, so nothing stopping you from enjoying her wares."

Colt slowly turned his head to glare at Constantine, not willing to ignore the way he was talking about Miss Reeves.

"I beg your pardon?" His voice came out more like a growl, and as he spoke, Layne reached his hand out and put it on his arm, ready to stop him from fighting if needed.

"Now, Brown, I'm not gonna let you stand here and talk about Miss Reeves like that. If'n you don't got anything nice to say, you can just pick up your feed and be on your way." Old Tom looked like even he was ready to punch the much younger man between the eyes.

"I'm not saying anything that isn't true, and you all know it. Why would a rich woman, who a man would have to be blind not to see her beauty, come all the way out here to the middle of nowhere if she didn't have every intention of scooping herself up a man? Wouldn't be the first time a rich city girl thought it would be some kind of romantic fun to marry someone beneath her, would it, Hammond?"

Colt swallowed hard, determined not to let this man get to him. But every time his heart beat in his chest, he could feel the blood pounding in his head. He didn't even realize he was straining to move toward Brown until Layne's fingers dug deeper into his arm.

"Don't do anything you'll regret, Colt. He isn't worth the time of day."

Thankfully, at that moment, Mrs. Brown walked back across the dusty street from the mercantile. She was a smart woman, and from the look on her face, she knew something was going on between the men. Her cheeks flushed with embarrassment, probably knowing full well her husband was causing trouble again.

Her smile faltered when she looked at the men in front of her, but she tried not to let anyone notice her shame. "I was thinking of asking Miss Reeves over for tea one day this week when the children aren't in school. Could you pass the message on to her, please? Tell her to stop by whenever she has some time and I'll be sure to welcome the visit."

Colt's eyes lifted in time to see the smirk on Constantine Brown's face. "Yes, you tell the young schoolteacher she's always welcome out at our place. Any time."

The way the man spoke the words sent chills down Colt's spine. He knew beyond a doubt there was no way he would ever let Miss Reeves go over there alone.

When he looked back at Mrs. Brown, he offered her a smile, but he could see the humiliation and hurt in her gaze. She'd heard the tone in her husband's voice but was pretending otherwise. "I'll be sure to let her know. And, if you ever want to come over to our place, you're always welcome. *Any time.*" Colt's eyes met hers as he spoke the last two words in echo of the other man's.

Except in this case, Colt hoped she'd pick up on the invitation that if she needed to get away from her husband at any time, she was welcome, day or night. Colt had noticed the dark circles under her eyes and seen enough bruises throughout the months she'd been here to know she didn't live a good life. If he could figure out a way to help her, he would, but for now this was all he could offer.

He helped her up into the wagon and watched them drive back out of town, her back perfectly straight as she bounced on the seat beside her husband.

"That poor woman."

Old Tom's words hung in the air as they waited for the dust to settle around them from the retreating wagon that was now past the bridge and headed down the road toward home. As he continued to watch, the wagon came to a stop beside someone walking along the edge of the road.

His stomach dropped when he realized it was the new schoolteacher they'd just been discussing.

He swore under his breath and hopped up onto the seat of his wagon without even saying a goodbye to the men left standing there. While he didn't want to discourage a friendship between Miss Reeves and Mrs. Brown, the last thing he wanted was for her to be anywhere near Constantine Brown.

It wasn't because he was jealous or anything. It was nothing more than general concern.

Brown wasn't good news, and he'd have to keep a close eye on Miss Reeves to make sure she was kept safe from him.

CHAPTER 8

Kathryn let her gaze follow the horizon, where as far as she could see beyond the newly plowed fields, long prairie grasses were blowing in the gentle breeze. The ride back to the ranch wouldn't take long, and she tried to swallow her disappointment that the rest of the walk she'd been so looking forward to after her first day of school had been taken from her. She'd walked into town, enjoying the warm sun kissing her cheeks as she'd soaked up the peaceful sounds of the world around her.

But, instead of being able to enjoy the leisurely stroll back home to end her perfect day, Mr. Hammond had come bouncing up in a large cloud of dust while she'd stood talking with their neighbors. He'd insisted he'd give her a ride back out to the farm after she'd run her errands, even when she'd been quite clear she could make her way back home on her own.

"I really didn't mind the thought of walking back to the farm. I only came into town to pick up the few necessities I needed, and to mail the letter to my sister." The last thing she wanted Mr. Hammond to feel was that he had to look after her all the time. She was perfectly capable of looking after herself out here.

"Well, I was coming this way anyway."

For some reason, Kathryn almost got the feeling he was angry about something. In all her days, she was sure she'd never met a moodier man than Mr. Colt Hammond.

And yet, after talking with Fae at the party, she'd been made to believe he was a kind, gentle, and caring man. While she'd noticed he was that way with his children and his mother, he'd surely never given her any glimpses of that personality toward her.

"The children did so well today in school. Delia is smart as a whip and her imagination never stops making me smile. She fits right in with the other kids in the classroom. Owen was still a bit unsure of everything and kept pretty much to himself, but I'm sure with time he will come around. He didn't really want to do any of the work I assigned him."

Kathryn wasn't sure how to bring it up with Mr. Hammond, so she just decided to tell him the truth. If he was going to be grumpy with her anyway, she had nothing to lose by mentioning the concern she had about his son.

He turned to face her and from under the large brim of her hat, his dark eyes held hers. "Was he causing any trouble?"

"No! No, nothing like that. He just seems so withdrawn. I was hoping you might have some ideas for me to get through to him. He's a wonderful child, and I know with time he's going to be just fine." The last thing she wanted to do was get Owen into trouble with his father.

He faced back toward the road, and Kathryn let the breath go she'd been holding. She'd seen such concern and love in those eyes for his son, and for a brief moment, she wondered if he'd ever looked at a woman with that same intensity before.

With a quick shake of her head, she came to her senses. Of course he had. He was a married man, so there must have been a time he'd shared that kind of love with his wife. Even if she wasn't here anymore.

And it wasn't like it was any of Kathryn's business anyway.

"Ever since his mother left, he's been struggling a bit. He seems to be all right with some people, but I notice he's different around women sometimes." He quickly looked at her, and she could see the sadness in his eyes before he turned away again. "I'll talk to him."

"No, don't say anything to him just yet. I'm sure it was just first day nerves. Give me some time to show him I'm someone he can trust."

He sighed and shook his head. "That's the thing. He likely knows you're not going to be around for a long time, so he's not going to let himself get too attached to you. So, don't give him any false hope. Otherwise, he'll just end up being worse off than he is now. Just let me talk to him and make sure he knows that it's never proper to be disrespectful to a lady, even if you aren't sure you can trust her."

Kathryn's mouth dropped open in disbelief. "Do you honestly think the way you're speaking to me right now isn't disrespectful? How can you expect him to learn any better when you're doing the same thing? Just because you don't seem to believe I'm going to stay here, it doesn't mean you can keep bringing it up and then wonder why your son won't give me a chance either."

She was shaking with anger now and was glad to see they were already driving up the lane toward the house. She didn't even wait for the wagon to come to a complete stop before she stood up, desperate to get away from the man who had her so furious.

When the wagon did finally lurch to a stop, she was already lifting one leg to step over the side. Before she could even comprehend what was happening, she was hurtling forward and landing in a heap on the hard ground.

As she lay face down in the dirt, she closed her eyes and groaned. She wasn't in any pain, but the humiliation of what she'd just done wasn't letting her move. All her life, she'd been quick to act without thinking, and this was one more time she'd let her anger take over.

Footsteps made their way to her and she wished the ground would just open up right there and swallow her. Without looking up, she knew Colt had come around the wagon and was standing there looking down at her. Most people would be concerned and try to help her up, instead of just leaving her in a pile of skirts on the ground.

"You know, while I'm sure your way is much quicker, using the step is generally a lot safer way of getting out of the wagon. Or, like most women, waiting until it's come to a complete stop and allowing a gentleman to help her down."

She pushed herself up into a sitting position, not looking at him as she dusted the arms of her blouse. Her basket filled with sugar, tea, and other small items she'd picked up was overturned with all the goods strewn around her.

"Well, if I'd have thought there was a gentleman around to assist me down, I might have waited."

His chest rumbled with laughter as he reached his hand down to her. How could this man go from making her so angry she could have pushed him from a moving wagon, to looking down at her with such a charming smile? Honestly, she was sure she'd never met anyone so exasperating in her life.

"Miss Reeves, are you all right?" The sound of the front porch door slamming reached her ears as Delia raced down the steps as fast as her little legs would take her. Mrs. Hammond was right on her heels, still holding onto a towel she'd obviously been using inside the kitchen when they'd pulled up.

As if her humiliation wasn't already bad enough, of course the entire family had witnessed her predicament. Now, if she refused his outstretched hand, she would look rude.

He was still grinning widely, obviously aware of her discomfort. As soon as his fingers closed over hers, heat went through her entire body, and by now she was sure her cheeks would soon ignite. He gave her a gentle tug and helped her stand up, holding onto her hand for a few seconds longer to make sure she was steady.

"I've been accused of many things in my life, but being a gentleman isn't one of them, I'm afraid." His voice was low enough just for her to hear, and she had to ignore the tingle it sent through her.

"I'll help you pick your things back up to put in your basket." Delia was down on the ground quickly rounding everything up.

"Oh, my dear. Are you all right?" By now, Mrs. Hammond was standing beside them, and she reached out to take Kathryn's hand. She patted it into the crook of her arm and turned to lead her into the house.

"I'm fine, Mrs. Hammond. I just got a little off balance. I think my pride is hurt worse than anything else."

The kind older woman stopped to send a stern look in her son's direction. "Colt Hammond. What kind of man are you to let a woman step out of a wagon on her own?"

Colt rolled his eyes and shook his head. "Mother, I know you would be watching out the window the minute you heard the wagon come up the road. So, don't pretend you didn't notice Miss Reeves standing up before I stopped. I assure you; I would have offered my assistance if she'd waited."

Mrs. Hammond wasn't paying any attention to her now exasperated son as she continued to pull Kathryn up the steps, with Delia right behind them carrying her basket.

It took everything Kathryn had not to laugh out loud at the look on his face when she dared to peek back at him one last time. Even though it didn't take the sting of her embarrassment completely away, seeing him chastised by his mother for something even Kathryn was willing to admit wasn't his fault, did make her feel somewhat better.

Now, she just needed to get through supper

with the family, and she could make her way back to her cabin and try to forget everything that happened in the past ten minutes.

But somehow, with the fact that her hand still tingled from where he'd held it, Kathryn knew forgetting it all was going to take a lot longer than it should.

CHAPTER 9

"*P*lease, can I go and stay the night with Miss Reeves? I can help to show her everything and then she wouldn't be all alone out there."

Colt looked down at his daughter who was pleading with him. They had finished supper, and he had offered to walk Kathryn back to her cabin. Delia had immediately started begging to spend the night with her new teacher.

His daughter had always been good at picking up on people's feelings, and Colt suspected she'd sensed Kathryn's nervousness about being at the cabin on her own. During supper, she'd asked a lot of questions about how to do certain things, and he realized they hadn't really given her much

62

instruction for a woman coming from a life of luxury in the city before leaving her to fend for herself down there.

"No, Delia, Miss Reeves needs her privacy. You can't be inviting yourself to stay with her."

Delia's face fell in disappointment at his words and she timidly looked toward Miss Reeves who was standing by the door holding the basket she'd brought back from town.

"Oh, it really wouldn't be any trouble for her to stay, if you'll allow it. Truthfully, I would welcome someone to keep me company and give me some help. I'm afraid my upbringing didn't involve the use of outside pumps for water or having to use a wood stove or anything like that on my own. I'm a bit embarrassed to admit it but having Delia with me for a night or two would actually be quite helpful to me."

Colt sensed that she might even be more nervous on her own than she was admitting to. His eyes stayed on her as she smiled down at Delia. Guilt hit him when he once again noticed the dirt on her skirt from her earlier fall. He knew she'd been angry with him, but he reminded himself it really wasn't his fault she'd fallen. If she'd have waited until he'd come to a complete stop and helped her down, it wouldn't have happened.

"Well, in that case, you can stay with her, Delia, as long as you promise not to bother her and to go to bed on time." His daughter was already squealing with excitement as she ran toward the stairs to go up and get the things she would need.

Miss Reeves looked out the window, and Colt followed her eyes to where Owen was out feeding the horses in the pen.

"I hope he doesn't think I'm favoring his sister by letting her stay with me. I mean, he could come and stay too, but I wouldn't have any place for him to sleep and I'm sure he wouldn't want to anyway."

Colt walked over and took his hat off the hook by the door, pushing it down hard on his head. "He'll be fine. In fact, he'll likely welcome a break from his sister for a bit. They're together all the time, so this will be a good chance for him to just have some time to himself."

"And I promise I'll sit him down to do his homework after he's finished his chores." Mrs. Hammond walked over to give Kathryn a hug. "Delia might try staying awake a little longer than she's supposed to, so you'll have to be firm with her. She's quite taken with you, though, so I'm sure she'll listen to anything you tell her to do."

The little girl bounded down the stairs with her nightgown and school dress for tomorrow folded neatly in her arms. Her reading book was placed on top, along with a well-loved stuffed bear. "I remembered my good dress to wear tomorrow. I didn't want to have to wear my dirty old chore clothes to school."

Miss Reeves laughed and took Delia's outstretched hand. "No, that would never do. Although I have to say you look quite beautiful in any dress you wear."

Colt was grateful for her words to Delia. Sometimes, he felt such guilt knowing his kids might not have all the finest clothes to wear, as his wife had been so quick to point out all the time. But, around here, most children made do with what their parents could afford so it wasn't something people thought much about.

He knew that people from the cities, especially women like Arlene and Miss Reeves, didn't understand the hardships and sacrifices people out here on the frontier had to make. He wondered what she would say if she knew the "chore dress," as Delia called it, was made from a flour sack.

They walked outside and down the steps, with Delia skipping along beside her teacher, still holding her hand. Something inside of Colt clenched at the sight, and he knew how much his daughter had missed having a mother. Anger at his wife started to bubble just beneath the surface and he quickly looked away before anyone noticed.

A little girl shouldn't have to grow up without a mother to care for her. His eyes found Owen who was throwing hay out for the horses in the small pen beside the barn. He knew his son was having a hard time too, but Colt just didn't know how to bring it up and talk to him about it.

"You really don't have to walk me home. I've got Delia to keep me company, and it's not far. I'm sure we would be all right."

"I said I'd walk you home, so that's what I'm going to do." Immediately he regretted how angry his words had come out. He clenched his jaw and looked straight-ahead, hoping no one else had noticed.

The silence that accompanied them as they made their way down the path toward the cabin assured him they had.

He looked over at Miss Reeves and offered her an apologetic smile. "Sorry about your dress. I'm sure you'll be able to get the dirt out of it when you wash it. Ma always does her washing on Monday's down at the creek, but I can ask her to do some things on Saturday so she can show you how."

He hoped she'd understand his apology was for more than her dusty dress. Her eyes met his for a moment and she shrugged. "Well, at least it didn't tear. I guess I need to remember to stay sitting until a wagon has come to a complete stop."

"Daddy says I'm always supposed to wait to let him help me down, because it isn't lady-like to be hopping over the side of the wagon. You should just wait for him to help you next time."

Colt pulled his lips tight to stop from smiling at the fact his innocent daughter had just told her teacher what she'd done wasn't considered lady-like. He knew Miss Reeves enough by now to know she would never scold Delia over her words, but he still moved his gaze back to her to see what her reaction was going to be.

Her mouth had opened, then closed, and when her eyes fell back on his, she burst out laughing. He couldn't remember the last time he'd heard anything so beautiful.

"You're absolutely right, Delia. I should have waited for help. I have so much to learn about living out here, so I'm very thankful to have a young lady like you to help me and make sure I'm not doing anything unseemly."

As they got closer to the cabin, Colt's heart jolted in the realization he was going to have to protect his daughter from being hurt again. He could already see how much she'd fallen for Miss Reeves, and he knew it was more than the feeling a student had for their teacher. She was trying to replace what she was missing in her life.

But Colt knew the woman wasn't going to stay, and he couldn't bear the thought of Delia having to go through the pain of losing her too. He reminded himself that he'd need to talk with Miss Reeves and tell her to make sure Delia didn't get too attached.

And, with a sudden sinking in his stomach, he knew it was something he'd have to be careful with too. She was far too easy to be around, making him feel things he didn't think he'd ever feel around a woman again.

But he was a grown man, so he knew he could take care of himself. He wasn't like a child, completely naive to what would eventually happen when she left.

No, he would be just fine. There wasn't a

woman alive who could make him believe she could be trusted.

Even one who was now bent over investigating a flower on the path with his daughter as though it was the most important thing in her life.

No, especially not her.

CHAPTER 10

"I don't see why I gotta help. This isn't man's work. Why can't I just go help pa in the field?"

Mrs. Hammond finished dumping the last bucket of creek water into the tub, then set it down on the ground and turned to face her grandson. "Owen Hammond, you know your pa wouldn't want to hear you talking like that about lady's or man's work. Sometimes a body has to do whatever they can to help, regardless of whether or not they think it's work they need to be doing."

Owen scowled and caught Kathryn's eye before he turned away and kicked at a stone on the ground. But not before she'd noticed the redness in his cheeks. She knew he was embarrassed being scolded by his grandmother in front of her, but even though he was ill-mannered at times, Kathryn understood. She really didn't know what she could do to make things easier for him, though. Owen seemed determined today to argue with everyone and just be grumpy to anyone who tried to talk to him. His father was plowing a bit more of the land, hoping to plant more crops there next spring, and had asked Owen to help his grandma and her carry water for their laundry.

Kathryn had been relieved to see that she wouldn't actually have to crouch down in the creek like she'd been imagining. Instead, they'd carried a tub down next to it where a small stand had been built to set it on to make washing clothes easier. Delia had been so proud to point it out to her, saying that some families still just washed their clothes right in the creek, but they didn't have to do that anymore.

Kathryn didn't have the heart to tell the little girl that this was still quite primitive to what she'd had back home. In truth, she hadn't actually ever washed her own clothes before, so she was nervous that it was going to be painfully obvious to everyone else just how much she didn't know.

"Now, in the colder months, we wash our

clothes up at the house. But in the summer, we do them out here so we don't heat the house up any more than it is. Besides that, I much prefer being down here at the creek, instead of having to haul buckets of water up. When winter comes, we just use well water or melt some snow on the fire."

Mrs. Hammond lifted the wicker basket she'd used to bring all of their clothes down to the creek and carried them over to where another tub was sitting on a large iron grate over a roaring fire. "We wash all the whites first, by letting them sit in some boiling water before taking them over to the washboard. Then we wash any colors, and the last ones are Colt's dirty work clothes." She smiled over at Kathryn. "But you just have your few clothes, so I would think you can even get away with only washing your things every two weeks."

"Well, I appreciate you taking your Saturday to show me how to do this. I know your regular laundry day is Monday."

Mrs. Hammond nodded as she threw more white clothing into the boiling tub. "Yes, it works best to do it on Mondays because sometimes it takes a few days for clothing to dry completely in the colder months, so it gives me time to also do any mending and the ironing before everyone needs their Sunday best."

Kathryn watched in admiration as the woman so matter-of-factly talked about her chores. They were such a part of her life that she barely even had to think about them anymore. But Kathryn knew how hard these everyday chores were in reality, even if these hardened frontier women had grown accustomed to them. She thought about her own mother, and knew without a doubt, these were tasks she would never be able to handle.

Life out here was so different from what Kathryn had grown up with, and for a brief second, the familiar doubts started to nudge her. But she quickly pushed them away and bent down to lift her own basket up. She walked over and threw her few white items into the boiling water.

"There, now while we wait for those to be ready to rinse, we will fill these buckets back up and set them near the fire to warm. It's better to do the scrubbing in warm water so our hands don't get too cold."

Kathryn worked alongside her, with Owen and Delia helping as much as they could. She was sure she would never understand how the older woman ever managed to do all of this on her own every week. Between moving the wet, heavy clothing between tubs and then actually wringing the water out of them, Kathryn was quickly exhausted. But she didn't want to let on to Mrs. Hammond because she knew the older woman would just tell her to rest and would finish it on her own.

Kathryn was determined this was a chore she would learn to do, and do it well enough that she wouldn't need anyone to help her. If she planned to live out here on her own, she had to be able to do these basic tasks.

"When can I come back and stay with you, Miss Reeves? It was so much fun, wasn't it? I can still smell the nice perfume you let me spray on my school dress, even though it was already three days ago."

Kathryn smiled over at Delia crouched down at the creek beside her filling up a bucket. The little girl tried to fill it all the way to carry it like the rest of them, but she was so small it almost tipped her over whenever she tried to walk.

"Delia, didn't your pa tell you not to be inviting yourself to Miss Reeves's house anymore? You mind your manners."

"It's fine, really, Mrs. Hammond. I don't mind. I enjoyed having the company for the nights she stayed." She looked at Delia and smiled. "But you always must obey what your pa tells you, isn't that right? I promise, one day soon I'll invite you down to stay again."

The girl had spent two nights with Kathryn, and she was the first one to admit just having someone else there had taken some of the fear out of the darkness outside her window at night. She knew she was being silly, and there wasn't really anything to worry about, but after growing up under the glow of the city streetlights at night, she hadn't ever imagined how dark the world around her would be without them.

Delia had informed her the first night she stayed that the awful howling and yipping sounds outside her window were just coyotes. She said they wouldn't hurt them unless they were sick or hungry, but Kathryn wasn't sure she believed her. Likely, it was just something her father had told the child to keep her from being scared of them.

Kathryn sat for a moment after the others lifted their buckets to carry back up the embankment, looking at her reflection in the water trickling past her.

In the clear depths, she could see dirt smudged around her eye, and many strands of hair poking out through the kerchief Mrs. Hammond had insisted she wear to keep it all pulled back while they worked. She didn't recognize the woman staring back at her, and she realized that within just a short week, she'd already changed from the girl she'd been growing up. She was proud of how she'd handled this first chance to be independent, even if she did look a little dusty and work-worn.

Dipping her fingers in the water, she leaned slightly forward to get a better look at the dirt on her face and reached up to wipe at it. The ripples in the creek made it hard to see, but if she just got down a little bit closer...

"You're going to fall in."

The words spoken loudly behind her startled her, and her foot slipped on the rock she'd been crouching on. Before she had a chance to even blink, she was lying face down in the cold water. She quickly jumped up, screaming as she reached up to push the wet hair that had escaped and flopped down into her face as she struggled to see.

Her eyes locked on Colt's shocked face staring back at her from the bank, just as her feet slipped out from under her again on the wet uneven creek bed beneath her. This time, she was sure her legs went straight in the air before her backside landed on a hard, cold rock, sending shooting pain through her entire body.

She barely noticed the splash of the water as it covered her completely. Gasping for air, she sat up and struggled to get back onto her feet, but no matter how hard she tried, her slippery shoes wouldn't grip on anything underneath her. The weight of her dress and underclothes weighed her down, making her attempts even more difficult.

Just when she was about to plunk herself down in the middle of the creek in defeat, she glanced up and saw Colt stepping into the water with his arms outstretched to grab her. She wasn't completely sure, but by the smirk on his face, it seemed he was fighting to hold back his laughter. She was immediately reminded of just a few days ago when she'd clumsily fallen out of the wagon and needed his assistance too.

This was not the impression of an independent and confident woman she'd been hoping to send to the people of this community. But at least she could be thankful it seemed to only happen in front of him.

"Stop flailing and take my hand!"

"I'm not flailing!"

Even as she said it, she knew she was, but she

was suddenly feeling extremely embarrassed and angry. Never in her life had she been clumsy, and now it seemed like she couldn't do anything without making a scene.

Finally, he grabbed her roughly by the arm and dragged her to standing, then pulled her onto the bank where the children and their grandmother were watching in horror as she'd carried on as though she was surely going to drown.

In less than a foot of water.

"You need to be more careful, Miss Reeves." Poor little Delia ran over and threw her arms around her soaking wet skirt.

Kathryn glared at Mr. Hammond. "Well, if people didn't sneak up behind others when they were leaning over open water, things like that wouldn't happen."

He raised an eyebrow and was definitely struggling not to laugh. "I really didn't sneak up behind anyone. I assumed you'd seen me coming, or at the very least, heard me speaking to the children when I arrived."

She'd been so lost in her thoughts, she hadn't even heard him. She let go of Delia and smiled reassuringly at the child as she stepped back and stared up at her with big, scared eyes.

Kathryn wasn't going to fight with her father in front of her, so she just reached down and started wringing out her skirt. She could only imagine the mess she looked like right now, and suddenly, her eyes burned from the tears that were threatening.

The last thing she wanted was for anyone to see her break down. "Mrs. Hammond, I'm going to run back to my cabin to get dry clothes on. I'll be back shortly, so just leave any of my clothes that are left to wash, and I'll finish when I'm dried off."

She couldn't even look at the kind older woman because of the worry she knew she'd see in her eyes. She just needed to get back to her cabin.

As she walked away as fast as she could without being in a full run, she could hear Mrs. Hammond scolding her son once again.

And as much as Kathryn would love to stop and turn back so she could hear Colt Hammond getting put in his place by his mother, the embarrassment of everything that had happened wasn't worth it.

Something about that man caused her to act like a dithering fool, and she was determined from this point forward to stay as far away from him as she could.

CHAPTER 11

"*M*iss Reeves said she's just going to have supper at her own place. She says she's quite tired from all the work today, but said to make sure I thank you for the offer."

Delia struggled to catch her breath after racing back up to the house from the cabin. She warily looked toward her father who was leaning against the fireplace mantle. "Do you think she's mad at you?"

Colt rolled his eyes as he shook his head at his daughter. "Of course not. Miss Reeves told you she was tired. I'm sure all the manual labor she had to do today did play her out. It's not like she'd be used to any kind of work like that."

Even as he said it, he did feel a twinge of guilt

thinking his daughter could perhaps be right. Although he wasn't sure why the woman would be mad at him, even though his mother had scolded him soundly after Miss Reeves had left to change into dry clothes.

He'd offered to wait and apologize when she returned to finish her laundry at the creek. But he'd been told in no uncertain terms to make sure he had gone back to his own chores before then. He couldn't remember the last time his mother had been so angry with him.

Now, as he met her eyes where she stood at the entryway into the small kitchen, he knew she was still fuming.

"Colt Hammond. Now look what you've done."

He let out an exasperated sigh. "Would you please explain to me what I've done? I don't understand how Miss Reeves falling into the creek is reason for everyone to be so upset with me."

"Son, you know I love you, but you can be a complete dim-witted fool sometimes."

She turned and walked into the kitchen, leaving him standing with his mouth hanging open. He knew even if he lived to be a hundred, he would never understand how a woman's mind worked.

"Delia, you run back outside and tell your

brother to come in and wash up for supper. I think he's out behind the barn with the new foal."

"Yes, Pa." She looked toward the kitchen, then back at him with a worried look as though she knew he was in trouble for something.

"Don't worry about me. I can handle your grandmother. I'm a grown man." He winked at his daughter, and she giggled before running out the door.

He wished he truly felt as brave as he'd acted. One thing he'd learned the hard way as a young boy was not to push his mother too far. She'd never laid a hand to him, but she had a look that would strike fear into even the toughest of men.

"So, do you want to explain to me exactly what I've done? I simply walked down to the creek to say hello to my family, a woman falls into the water, and suddenly everyone wants to hang me up by my britches."

His mother turned around from the counter where she was ladling the stew into the bowls. "She didn't just fall into the water, and you know it. You walked up and startled her."

He put his hands out and lifted his shoulders in an exaggerated shrug. "And how is that my fault?"

"You know full well you've been stomping

around and doing everything you can to prove that she doesn't belong out here. And don't even try denying it. I've seen how you've been acting."

"Well, just because I don't believe she'll cope with life here, it doesn't mean I walked up behind her and deliberately scared her, hoping she'd fall into the creek." He walked over to lift a biscuit off the plate, but his mother slapped his hand away. "The way you're all acting, you'd think I went over and pushed her."

His mother turned and faced him with her hands on her hips. She held the wooden ladle in one hand, and the thick gravy dripped onto her clean apron.

"If you'd seen that poor girl when she came back to finish her work, you'd understand why I'm so angry. She was embarrassed, and no matter how much I tried to assure her that she wasn't the first to fall into the creek doing laundry, she wouldn't believe me."

"She also fell out of the wagon a few days ago, Mother. Don't you remember? I can't really help it if the woman is a bit clumsy."

"Colt, do you not think perhaps she's just trying so hard to prove that she belongs here, that maybe, just maybe, she ends up a little flustered at times? In the schoolroom, there is absolutely no doubt she's in her element and where she belongs. The children in this town already love her. But she knows she has a lot to learn about living on the frontier, but bless her, at least she is trying."

He knew Delia couldn't say enough nice things about her teacher every day when she got home from school, and everyone he'd spoken to in town had nothing but praise for how much their children were enjoying school.

But that was as far as her "skills" went.

"Mother, I just don't think it's a good idea for all of these children to get too attached to a woman who will never last even a few more weeks out here. I'm just being realistic. Even her clothing won't be able to withstand life on the frontier. Did you see the skirt she was wearing today? It was made from better material than your best Sunday dress."

His mother hadn't taken her eyes off his face. "Is it the children you're really worried about, Colt?"

He clenched his jaw tight and ignored the sudden pounding in his chest. He loved and respected his mother more than anyone in this world, but he wasn't going to let her make insinuations that weren't true.

"Why don't you just say what you're getting at?"

"Colt, I watched what happened with Arlene. I spent those years watching as she became a bitter, horrible woman to you, but you still kept believing she could learn to love living here as much as you did. I sat back while she almost convinced you to give everything up that you love here to move to a city where she could live more *civilized*." Her voice softened and she came over closer. "Thankfully, she didn't succeed. I hate to think about what could have happened."

"Well, that's all done and over. And it has nothing to do with Miss Reeves falling in the creek." He wasn't in the mood to discuss his past failures with his mother right now.

Her hand reached out and landed on his arm before he could turn away. "Not every woman from the city is like Arlene. That's all I'm saying. Give Miss Reeves a chance to prove she can manage out here. You have to see that she's at least trying, and that's more than your wife ever did."

Thankfully, the screen door slammed, and Delia ran into the kitchen with Owen right behind her.

"Is Miss Reeves leaving, Pa?" Owen's voice sounded almost relieved.

"No, she's not leaving. Why would you say that?" Colt looked between his children, and while his son seemed happy with the thought, Delia looked devastated. Her eyes dropped to take sudden interest in her boot.

"Delia said Miss Reeves was upset about falling in the creek today and likely won't want to stay anymore."

Colt took a deep breath and shut his eyes. He reached up and pinched the bridge of his nose as he had a sudden pounding in his head. "Miss Reeves isn't going anywhere. She's not just upset about falling in the creek. And I will go and talk to her."

He was sure there had never been a time in his life when he was more confused about what had happened than this very moment. Honestly, a woman falls into a little bit of water and the whole world goes crazy.

And now, he was going to have to go apologize to her for doing nothing more than walking up behind her.

He'd never been a drinking man, but days like this, he wished he was.

CHAPTER 12

"Oh, Miss Reeves, I just can't tell you how much it means to me watching my Hazel learning her letters already. She just thinks the world of you. I'm glad she's going to have better opportunities than I had. I've always wanted to learn to read."

Kathryn smiled warmly at the kind woman in front of her who wouldn't be much older than herself. She had a bit of an accent, but Kathryn wasn't sure where it was from. Her aunt had told her there were a lot of immigrants living on farms around Promise, so it wasn't unusual.

"If you ever want to learn, let me know. I'd be more than willing to teach you." Even though an education was something Kathryn had always taken for granted, she knew it was a privilege many women in some of the rural communities might not have. And she was determined not to ever make anyone feel embarrassed or ashamed of it, so she hoped they would feel comfortable letting her help if they were willing.

"Oh, it's too late for me to learn. But, just knowing my little girl will have better chances fills me with joy."

"Well, if you ever want to learn, please don't hesitate to ask. It wouldn't be any trouble, and I don't believe that it's ever too late for anyone to learn."

Kathryn turned as another woman came over to thank her for coming to teach in Promise. They'd arrived back at the Hammond's farm, where many of the folks from town were joining together for a picnic after the Sunday service. And ever since, the townspeople had been coming over to tell her how much of a difference she'd already made in just a week.

For the first time in her life, she truly felt like she had a purpose. Growing up with money was nice, but she'd always felt like she didn't have anything to offer that was something only she could give. These people in Promise didn't care about money. They cared more about family and friends, and just having the chance for something better for their children.

And this was the one thing she could give them.

After the week she'd had, she needed something to give her a boost. Teaching in the small one room school was everything she'd dreamed it would be, and the hours she spent inside those walls, teaching the children, filled her with happiness. But those hours seemed to go by so fast, and while the Hammond family had been generous by letting her come up there to take her meals all week, she knew she couldn't impose on their hospitality forever.

That meant she was going to have to learn to cook on the wood stove in her cabin, and she'd have to spend time on her own during the evening hours.

Last night had been dreadful. After she'd hastily told the Hammonds she was just going to take her meal by herself, she'd realized she didn't even have any food other than some bread that Mrs. Hammond had sent down two days prior.

Even if she'd had something to cook, she wouldn't have known where to start. Everything was so different from back home.

Her stomach had rumbled all through the morning's service, and she prayed that the Hammonds would invite her to join them to eat after. On the way into church this morning, everyone had seemed so quiet, but Delia had mentioned something about a few of the families coming out to their place after the service for a picnic.

Her pride might have got in the way last night, but today, Kathryn was willing to beg for the chance to have a proper meal if she had to.

Her gaze moved toward Mr. Hammond who was standing near the wagons talking with some of the men. As though he knew she was looking, his eyes turned and met hers. Quickly, she focused back on the woman who was now talking to her.

Why did her face suddenly feel so warm?

She knew why. She was embarrassed at how upset she'd gotten over falling in the water. And the worst part was, she didn't even know why she had been so angry.

He hadn't done it on purpose, and even though she hadn't come right out and yelled or gotten angry with him, it had been pretty obvious to everyone that she was upset about what happened.

And then she hadn't joined them for supper, so

she cringed as she imagined what they might have had to say about it all.

If only she'd just dusted off her pride and gone back to the creek like nothing had happened. Instead, when she'd gone back, poor Mrs. Hammond had felt terrible and tried to make her feel better, while Kathryn would have preferred to not even talk about it.

Mr. Hammond had barely spoken more than a few words to her today, but he hadn't brought up anything about yesterday.

And she was hoping he would keep it that way.

Finally, the woman moved on, leaving Kathryn standing alone. Her stomach made a loud noise again, and she was so grateful no one was around to hear it.

"Either you've swallowed a live duck, or I'd say maybe your stomach might be trying to tell you it needs something to eat."

She whipped around at the sound of Mr. Hammond's voice. He stood smiling innocently at her, while she was left wishing she could run back to the safety of her cabin and never face this man again.

"Do you ever do anything except sneak up behind people to insult them or scare them?"

"I was simply waiting until Mrs. Groves was finished talking to you so I wouldn't interrupt. I assumed you'd heard me coming. I'm starting to wonder if you should perhaps see old Doc Jacobs about your hearing."

She stared at him, biting her lip to keep from saying exactly what was on her mind.

Finally, he lifted his hands in surrender and laughed. "All right, I apologize. I can see you don't appreciate my attempts at humor."

Her mouth opened slightly but she still couldn't speak. He looked around uncomfortably as a few more wagons pulled into the yard, then pushed his hat back slightly and ran his fingers into his hair.

"I came over to tell you I'm sorry for startling you yesterday and causing you to fall into the creek. Instead, I end up making things worse." He finally looked back at her. "I'm likely a bit uncivilized compared to the men you grew up around, and I admit I'm not very good at being *proper*, or whatever you'd call it."

Something inside her let go, and she was able to take a good look at the man in front of her without feeling defensive.

His hair hung a bit long below the edge of the large brimmed hat he wore only for church. It was the exact same kind as the one he wore every other day but was much cleaner and not as worn.

His eyes were a dark color, and in the corners, the start of tiny crow's feet gave him the look of a man who had worked hard over the years but had also shared a lot of laughter.

She chuckled softly and shook her head as her hands came up to hug her stomach. "I accept your apology. And, in all fairness, I have likely made it quite hard to act very proper around. I mean, there aren't many women who literally fall out of a wagon, then a few days later end up in a creek in front of a man."

He grinned at her and nodded. "You forgot about the stomach noises loud enough to wake the dead."

She briefly clenched her eyes shut in embarrassment but couldn't hold in the laughter. "Right, I completely forgot about that. But, for future reference, a *proper* gentleman would never, ever point out anything as indelicate as a lady's body noises in public."

"Miss Reeves! Come sit over here with us. I've put our blanket under the big tree with my swing." Delia ran over to them and reached up to tug at her hand.

"Oh, I should really go help your grandmother get some of the food set out that she's prepared." Kathryn looked toward the house where a table had been set up for everyone to place their food on. Women were bustling around while children ran past toward the creek.

The day was warm and as she stood there watching these people who took each day a little bit slower, she knew she would never fit in back in the city again. This was the life she wanted to be a part of.

"Come on. Mother will already have everything ready. I think you better get some food in your stomach before you faint from hunger." He put his hand on her elbow to lead her behind the little girl who was skipping toward the tree with their blanket already placed neatly below it.

A sudden jolt of heat found its way through the thin fabric of her blouse and coursed through her entire body. She resisted the urge to pull her arm from his grasp, not wanting to let him see how much his touch could affect her.

Because, no matter what else happened, she needed to remember Colt Hammond was still a married man.

CHAPTER 13

*C*olt read over the words on the paper one more time, but with every letter his eyes took in, his vision started to blur with anger. His hands shook and he cursed low under his breath before taking the paper and folding it back up. He slammed it into his back pocket as he walked toward the mercantile where he'd left his wagon for Caleb to set the supplies into.

"Whoa there, Colt. You almost knocked me over."

The large, burly man he'd bumped into as he came around the front of the wagon reached out and took hold of his shoulder to steady him.

Colt wasn't in the mood for small talk, but he recognized him immediately as Mr. Charles

Ingalls, a man who lived over in De Smet. He sometimes came into Promise to pick up supplies that weren't available there. Many times, he would get items other people from De Smet needed and deliver to them.

"Sorry. Didn't see you there."

"No, I reckon you didn't." Mr. Ingalls walked past him and set something down on the back of his own wagon parked in front of Colt's. Colt couldn't believe he hadn't noticed it, but he guessed with the rage fueling his steps, he'd been preoccupied.

Mr. Ingalls turned back and looked at him intently. "Everything all right? You look like you've seen a ghost."

Caleb walked out of the mercantile with the large sack of flour to throw into his wagon, just in time to overhear the conversation. "I have to agree with Mr. Ingalls, here. Your face has a slight green tinge to it."

"I'm fine. Just wasn't paying attention."

The last thing he wanted to do was stand here and gossip about the mail he'd received. Soon enough, everyone in town would know anyway.

Mr. Ingalls kept his eyes on him, but he must have decided not to question it more. Nodding, he turned, hopping up onto the seat of his wagon and turned back to face them. "I forgot to congratulate you for getting the old school back up and running here in town. It will fill a great need for the community. I've heard the new teacher you've brought out is fitting in nicely."

Colt leaned against his wagon and shrugged. "She has a lot to learn about living out here, but I guess she's not doing too bad."

The man laughed. "Well, I'd reckon we all still have a lot to learn about living out here. The fact that she's here and willing to try is more than could be said for many." He flicked the reins and started the wagon moving. "It was nice to see you. You both take good care."

Colt stood still, watching until Mr. Ingalls was nothing more than a cloud of dust going down the road from town back toward De Smet. He was lost in his own thoughts and didn't even realize Caleb had come over to stand in front of him with his arms crossed.

"Are you going to tell me what has you looking like you're ready to kill the next person who so much as looks in your direction?"

"It's nothing that concerns you."

He knew he was being grumpy and rude, but

right now, he was having a hard enough time figuring everything out in his own head.

"I've known you most of my life, Colt. I know not much gets you ruffled, so obviously something's going on. You may as well tell me, because if you go home in the mood you're in, you're going to have to answer to your mother. And I think we both know how well that would end for you."

Sighing, Colt pushed himself away from the wagon and turned, leaning his arms over the back of it so he wouldn't have to face his friend as he spoke.

"Arlene has sent a letter asking me to file for a divorce."

The sounds of the town, with people going about their day, filled the air between them as Colt waited for Caleb's reaction. Getting a divorce was still considered to be a huge scandal around this town, even if the Dakota Territory was known as one of the divorce colony states where couples could come and live for a few months to obtain a divorce if desired. Most people who came to live for the mandatory three months were moving into the larger towns to spend their required time, so the small, rural areas like Promise were still not as accepting of the practice.

Finally, Caleb let out a low whistle. "The woman sure has nerve. But you had to have known something like this was going to happen. Why doesn't she just file the papers herself? The laws do allow for women to file, don't they?"

Colt swallowed the anger that was threatening to boil over. "She doesn't want to file. The scandal would be too much for her, so if I'm the one who does it, she can live the charade as the wounded woman who was abandoned by her husband."

"So, what if you don't file?"

His jaw hurt from clenching his teeth so hard as he growled out his reply, "If I don't, she says she'll come back and take the kids from me."

Caleb laughed bitterly. "She's never wanted those children. Why would she do that?"

"To force my hand." He turned back around to face his friend. "She's found another man she wants to marry. He's in the theater and travels with the shows she's a part of. She's in love, and if I don't give her the divorce, she's going to say I committed adultery and that's why she left. She says she'll smear my name all over to anyone who will listen and make sure the children end up going with her."

Caleb shook his head angrily. "She would never

make anyone believe that around here. Everyone knows what happened."

"Maybe. But the doubt will always be there for some. And I can't risk losing the children. If she wants a divorce, I'm more than happy to give it to her, if it means she'll be out of my life for good." He looked toward the bridge coming into town where Mr. Ingalls had left just a few moments ago. Another wagon was coming up the road.

"I just wish the children didn't have to grow up without a mother to love them. Every child deserves that much."

"Well, now that you'll have your freedom from Arlene, maybe it's time to consider finding someone who can help you raise them."

Colt rolled his eyes dramatically. "There's not a woman in the world worth the risk of getting married again."

Caleb was about to say more, but the wagon Colt had noticed earlier pulled up beside them, and he immediately cringed. He offered a sincere smile to Mrs. Mercy Brown as he reached his hand up to help her down, while her husband hopped down from the other side.

"Thank you, Mr. Hammond." Mercy smiled warmly at him, but he noticed the smile didn't reach her eyes. Dark shadows gave evidence to the sadness he was sure he could see in her face.

"Hurry up, woman. I haven't got all day to be hanging around in town while you gossip with Fae inside. Get your money for your eggs and get back out."

"But I told you I need some sugar today. Can I use the money to pick up a small bag, please?"

"No, we don't need anything like that. It's not like any amount of sugar can help make your food taste any better anyway." Constantine Brown looked to the other two men and laughed loudly. "Trust me to end up saddled with a woman who can't cook to save her life. Not like my ma used to do, anyway. And now that she's with child, she's thinking she can make excuses for getting outta some of her work."

Colt's mood quickly went from bad to worse as he saw the shades of red flood Mrs. Brown's cheeks. Her eyeballs were awash, but she held her head high and pushed her shoulders back before turning to go into the mercantile.

"What kind of man says words to humiliate his wife in front of others?" Colt could barely get the words out past the rage in his chest.

Caleb stepped over beside Colt and together

they faced Brown with their arms crossed in front of them.

"Oh, and you're any kind of man to be giving advice to me. At least I'm man enough to be sure my wife stays where she's meant to be."

No longer able to control his fury, Colt lunged at the other man, knocking him to the ground. Dust flew up all around them, and from what seemed like miles away, he could hear people hollering as his fist made contact with Brown's jaw.

But before he could take another swing, Caleb grabbed hold of his arm and stopped him. "He's not worth dirtying your boots or getting blood on your hands over."

Colt stayed sitting on top of the man who was bringing his hands up to cover his face. "So, it seems like you're sure quick to hand out insults and vile talk when it comes to a woman, but you're not up to facing off with another man."

"You jumped me! I didn't even have time to defend myself."

A crowd had gathered, and Colt lifted his eyes in time to see Mrs. Brown come rushing out of the store. Her horrified expression cut through his anger enough to allow him to stand, letting the other man get to his feet. Brown pulled his arm out of Caleb's grip and bent down to pick up his hat that had fallen off in the scuffle.

"No wonder your wife couldn't stand to be around you. You're a heathen. From now on, mind your own business and don't be stickin' your nose in where it don't belong." He hastily brushed the dust from his pants, then grabbed his wife's arm and dragged her to their wagon, forcibly pushing her up onto the seat. He hopped up beside her and grabbed the reins. "You're lucky you had your friend here to back you up. Might not be so lucky the next time we meet up."

Mrs. Brown gave Colt a sorrowful look before turning away as the wagon bounced away in a cloud of dust.

Colt wasn't in the mood to stand around and talk to Caleb or any of the others who had gathered around, so he went over to his own wagon and climbed into the seat.

Everything had gone wrong from the moment he pulled into town this morning, and while he had his own troubles to deal with, now Colt had a sickening feeling he'd just made things even worse for poor Mercy Brown.

CHAPTER 14

"All right, children. We're all finished for the morning, so you can get your lunch pails and go outside." Kathryn leaned against her desk and watched as the students jumped to their feet and ran out the door. She wiped her forehead with her hand, pushing the strands of hair back that had become matted to her skin.

It was a hot day and even with the windows open there was no relief. There was no breeze at all, leaving the room inside stuffy and warm, making it difficult for the children to concentrate. She was considering moving the class outside under the big tree for the afternoon where it might be a bit cooler, otherwise she was sure there wouldn't be much learning happening today.

She remembered from the few times she'd visited her aunt as a child how hot the summer days could get on the wide-open prairies. Even when there was a breeze, quite often the moving air was still warm and heavy, offering no relief until the sun was set for the day.

Grabbing the strawberry jam sandwich she'd made herself this morning, Kathryn made her way outside.

"Miss Reeves! Come sit with us!"

She smiled over at the group of young girls, including Delia and her friend Hazel, who'd called to her. They were sitting nicely beneath the big tree while the boys from the class were busy running around playing tag already. She would let them play for a few minutes more before telling them to sit down and eat their lunches too.

"It's not much cooler outside, is it? I was hoping there might be a breeze by now." She sat down and smiled at the girls who were all moving to make room for her. Already, she'd grown so attached to these children, and seeing the kindness they always showed to others, made her proud to have a hand in helping them grow.

Her legs were out to the side, so she spread her skirt out to make sure everything stayed covered.

She was sure both her mother and sister would be completely mortified if they saw her right now, sitting on the dusty ground without any thought to her clothing. But things were done differently out here, and she was already becoming so comfortable with the way of life, she never gave it much thought anymore.

The girls all chattered excitedly, seemingly completely unaffected by the heat. Kathryn smiled as she tried to keep up with the stories they were sharing. Just as she was taking the last bite of her sandwich, a loud commotion broke out over by the steps to the school.

"You're a no good, dirty weasel."

"Let go of me!"

"I said, take it back!"

She jumped to her feet as the loud, angry voices rose above the dust that was being thrown around as two boys scuffled on the ground.

It seemed like she was miles away as she raced over to break up the fight, and her heart sunk to her toes when she realized the boy on top, ready to throw his fist into the other boy's face, was Owen.

She made it just in time to grab his wrist and stop him. "Owen. Robert. Stop this!"

She pulled hard, lifting Owen off the other boy,

but as she did, Robert kicked his feet and connected with Owen's shin. He jerked his arm from her grasp and jumped back on top of the other boy, punching him in the shoulder.

"Boys! Enough!"

By now, all the children were standing around, the boys shouting and cheering them on, while the girls were screaming for them to stop.

Delia's terrified voice was the only one Kathryn could hear. She was pleading with her brother to stop, and Kathryn knew without looking that the young girl was crying.

Finally, with one last pull, she was able to get Owen back on his feet and a few steps away from Robert. Thankfully, one of the older boys in the class moved over to stop him from coming after Owen.

"Let go of me."

As Owen said the words, he quickly moved, loosening her hold, and making her lose her balance. She stumbled forward just as his arm swung around, his little fist slamming into her cheekbone.

In shock, she brought her hands up to ease the sting, but as soon as she saw the devastated look on Owen's face, any of her own pain quickly disappeared.

Before she could say anything, though, he turned and ran away.

"Owen, wait. Where are you going?" Delia tried to run after her brother, then stopped as Kathryn put her hand out to stop her.

"It's all right, Delia. I will go and talk to him."

"But…but…he hit you! Are you going to give him a whipping?"

The tear-soaked eyes pleaded with her not to hurt her brother.

"Delia, no! How could you ever think I'd do such a thing?"

Delia looked down at the ground, before shrugging. "Well, sometimes our ma would get mad at us. I don't think she liked us very much, though." Her eyes lifted and met Kathryn's. "But you like us, don't you?"

Kathryn didn't know whether to stay here and comfort the girl in front of her, or chase after the brother who had just run off. Not to mention, all the other children standing around uncertain of what to do.

Crouching down, she took Delia's hands in hers and smiled at her. "Sweetheart, I do like you.

And your brother. Very much. Nothing you could ever do would make me change my mind. And I most certainly would never hurt either of you." She squeezed the trembling hands tighter. "Now, I need you to stay here with your friends while I go talk to your brother, all right? Can you help to make sure no one gets into any trouble?"

Delia's eyes lit up at the thought of getting to be like the teacher for a few moments.

Kathryn stood up and faced the crowd of upturned faces. "You can continue playing outside for a while, or rest in the shade and read from your readers. Delia is in charge, so listen to her." She looked over at one of the older girls named Mary and gave a slight wink. Mary was a very well-behaved and mature girl, so Kathryn knew she would help to take care of everyone for the time she was gone.

Quickly, Kathryn started to follow in the path that Owen had taken. He'd gone the opposite direction from the house, headed toward the trees on the far side of the property.

What had happened to cause the boys to fight in the first place? Her heart pounded in her chest as fear gripped her. What if she couldn't find Owen? How was Mr. Hammond going to react when he heard what had happened? A good teacher shouldn't ever have let the kids get into a fight like that. She should have been paying better attention.

She slowly walked along the tree line, peeking into the bushier spots to see if Owen was hiding away in the thicker areas. Sweat dripped from the ringlets of hair that were now hanging all around her face. She pushed her sleeves up higher, not caring that every time she moved more branches aside, scratches were being left on her skin.

Finally, when she was certain she would have to run to the house and get his father, she could make out the faint sound of someone sniffling. She knew Owen was going to be terribly embarrassed for her to catch him crying, so she called out to let him know she was close.

"Owen, are you here?"

She moved one last branch and looked into the small hideaway inside the trees. Owen sat leaning against a tall tree in the middle, with his knees pulled up to his chin and his arms wrapped tightly around them.

She bent down to crawl in beside him, not paying any attention to the dirt beneath her.

"Do you mind if I come and sit in here with you? It's a beautiful little spot here."

She'd already figured out that this was a place he was familiar with when she noticed how well packed the ground was in the small area. And she could see where he'd moved some of the branches and twigs around to make it even more hidden away.

He didn't say anything as she sat down beside him. He kept his eyes looking down at his shoes while his chin rested on his knees. The redness in his eyes tore at her heart, knowing how much pain he was in.

Without thinking, she reached out and pulled him into her arms. She knew she should be scolding him for fighting, and finding out what had happened, but instincts told her that this boy just needed someone to hold him and love him.

So, that's what she did.

At first, the tension in the small body made it difficult, but after a few moments, he collapsed into her embrace. He leaned his head into her shoulder and let her arms go all the way around him.

"I'm sorry, Miss Reeves. I know I shouldn't have been fighting. And now I hit you, and you probably hate me. I know you'll want to leave, and it's all my fault."

"Owen! I could never hate you. Don't ever say that. And I'm not going anywhere over a silly little fight." She let her hand move over his soft hair, then leaned back and looked down into his eyes. "Do you want to tell me what you were fighting about?"

His throat moved as he swallowed hard, then he moved back into the same sitting position she'd found him in. She was sure he wasn't going to tell her anything, but he surprised her when he started to quietly speak.

"He said he heard his pa talking last night about my ma and how she ran off on us. Then he laughed and made fun of me because we must be pretty awful for a ma to not even love her own children, so I hit him."

Every word Owen spoke tore at Kathryn's heart. The pain and hurt she could hear in his voice broke her, so she just pulled him back into her arms and let him cry. It was something she sensed he'd needed to do for a long time.

"Owen, I don't know what happened with your ma, but I know without a doubt in my mind, that mothers love their children no matter what. But sometimes, life just doesn't work out the way we planned, and I'm sure it wasn't easy for your ma to leave. All I know is that you and Delia are wonderful children, and I know for a fact how much your pa loves you, and your grandma too." She pulled back and looked down into his tear-soaked eyes. "And nothing you did caused your ma to leave. Or Delia. You're not awful, and Robert is going to be punished for what he said to you."

He swallowed loudly. "Am I in trouble too?"

She smiled at him before nodding. "Well, I can't let you hit other children in school, even if you do think he deserved it. I'm going to have to keep you both after school for a bit today and you can help me wash the chalkboards and floors."

"I guess that's not too bad. Are you going to tell my pa?"

She could see the worry in his eyes.

"I'm afraid I have to let him know, Owen. But your pa will understand, and I'll tell him I've taken care of the punishment."

"But I hit you."

"It was an accident, Owen. I'm not mad."

"I'm really sorry. I didn't mean to hit you."

"I know. Sometimes accidents happen."

As she smiled down into his upturned face,

something shifted in the young boy's eyes. For the first time since she'd arrived in Promise, she didn't see complete despair in his face.

She'd finally broken through the shield he'd put up, and she was determined to pull him completely out of his shell and back into the happy child she knew he could be.

CHAPTER 15

*C*olt leaned over the basin and cupped his hands to bring the cold water up to his face. He closed his eyes and let the coolness soothe his skin, even knowing the heat from the day wasn't going to let the relief last for long.

He lifted his head and reached for the towel beside the window, while his eyes moved to watch the women outside.

During the heat of the summer, many days the women around here would go back to cooking their meals outside over a fire, using metal hooks to hang the pots on. Lighting a fire inside the house when it was so hot outside made it unbearable to live in, so while it might make the work a bit more difficult, most women preferred it this way.

He checked to make sure Owen had remembered to bring the buckets of water up to set beside the fire where his mother and Miss Reeves were cooking. His mother always made sure water was nearby to stop any sparks that may land on dry grass or, as had happened many times over the years, even onto the hem of her dress as she cooked.

His eyes moved to the young woman beside his mother. Kathryn had been coming up to the house right after her day of teaching every day for the past couple of weeks now, letting his mother show her how to cook on the frontier.

He knew how tired she must be trying to do it all, managing the children all day in school, then helping with the cooking and cleaning up after. And on Saturdays, she was out doing her laundry, just as his ma had taught her.

Of course, she always had Owen and Delia helping her, so he supposed it took some of the workload off her.

Ever since the day Owen had gotten in trouble for fighting at the school, he'd seemed to open up to Miss Reeves and had been nicer to her. Colt was glad he'd worked through some of the anger he'd obviously been feeling when the new teacher had first shown up, but at the same time, it worried him about what would happen now when she left.

He was sure Owen wanted to trust her, but he was still holding himself back a bit in case he started to care for her, and she decided to leave him too. Colt knew with Miss Reeves's personality, though, it was only a matter of time until Owen gave her his complete trust.

And he would be left devastated again, with Colt to pick up the pieces.

He finished drying his face, then walked out onto the porch, noticing how the sweat was already starting to drip from his neck again. The temperature had been high for days and if they didn't soon get some rain, he hated to think what would happen to all the crops in the fields.

"Miss Reeves, why don't you come sit down for a bit. I'm sure ma can manage now."

Her cheeks were a fiery red, and strands of hair hung down and stuck to her forehead from the heat. She turned at the sound of his voice and smiled, causing his breath to catch slightly.

How could a woman still be so beautiful even looking as ragged as she was at the moment?

Giving his head a shake, he swallowed hard and walked toward them.

"It's fine, Mr. Hammond. Your mother has been generous enough to teach me how to cook and survive on my own out here, so I'm going to do everything I can to help. It's the least I can do for everything your family has done for me since I arrived."

"I've asked you to please call me Colt. I've never been able to get used to being called mister. It makes me sound like an old man."

His ma scowled at him. "Now, young man. Your pa was well respected around here and many people addressed him as Mr. Hammond. There's nothing wrong with that."

"No, Ma. You're right. But it suited him better than it does me."

He caught the smile on Miss Reeve's face as she quickly turned back to stirring the pot of beans before replying, "Well, I've told you to call me Kathryn, and until you do so, I won't be using your given name either. It wouldn't be proper."

Colt sighed and shook his head. It was ingrained in him to address a woman by her correct title but even so, he said, "How many times do I have to tell you that out here on the frontier we aren't too worried about what's proper and what isn't."

"Colt Hammond. Just because you don't care about proprieties, it doesn't mean the rest of the folk around here don't."

He bent over and kissed his mother's cheek, feeling the heat that came off her reddened cheeks. He knew he shouldn't rile her up so much, but sometimes it was just too easy. "Ma, you're the most proper woman in the Dakota Territory. But even you have to admit we all have to make certain concessions out here that might not be acceptable in the cities back east."

"Well, you're right about that. I just don't think you should be encouraging everyone to become total heathens either just because we don't follow proper rules out here all the time."

He laughed and went over to sit on a stump he used for chopping wood. "Be careful you don't get too close to that fire, *Kathryn*. I see a spark just about landed on your skirt."

He made sure to emphasize her name to see his mother's reaction. But he was more shocked at his own reaction as the word had rolled off his tongue. It had seemed so intimate to call her by her given name, and something inside his chest clenched.

But the woman in front of him just laughed, completely unaware of his sudden discomfort as she patted at the fabric of her skirt. "I'm actually surprised I haven't completely burned my skirts. Until I came out here to live, I hadn't ever considered how dangerous cooking could be."

He held his breath when she looked back at him and smiled.

"Thank you, Mr....I mean, *Colt*. I should have changed into my other clothes after school today, but I was in a hurry because after we eat, I need to get back home and make my pies for the fair tomorrow. I brought the one I made last night for you all to try for supper tonight. Hopefully, they're getting better."

Along with the regular cooking his mother had been showing her, Kathryn had been determined to learn how to bake a pie after she'd heard about the upcoming fair to be held in Promise. Every year after the crops were all in the field, the community came together for a summer celebration where the kids could play, food was plentiful, and good-natured contests abounded to see who would take home the ribbon for the best pies, jams, and quilts.

In truth, it was just an excuse for the townsfolk

to be together, have some fun, and relax before the harvest season began.

And Kathryn had been practicing for days to make a pie to put into the contest and one to auction off. All money raised went to the church and she was hoping to have something to contribute.

But Colt was worried about the chances she would have to even get anyone to bid if they tasted any that she'd made to this point. He gave her credit for trying, because truthfully it was more than his wife had ever done when she moved out here. However, it didn't change the fact that the first few pies he'd tasted of Kathryn's had left him with nothing more than a great deal of pride in his own acting abilities. While he'd managed to swallow a few bites and convince her they weren't completely terrible, his children hadn't been able to hide their distaste as well as he had.

Thankfully, she seemed to know she wasn't as skilled in the kitchen as she would like, and had even laughed when the children had quickly spat their first bites back onto their plate.

She was getting better, and he'd managed to actually finish his last few pieces of pie she'd made this week, so he knew with time she would be every bit as good of a cook as his mother. She was the kind of woman who wasn't going to stop until she had learned something completely.

The only thing was, Colt didn't know if she'd be here long enough to get there.

CHAPTER 16

"Oh, my dear, your pies look absolutely wonderful. Your father would be so proud of you right now." Kathryn reached out to hug her aunt who had come over to greet her as soon as she'd spotted her setting her pies onto the judging table.

"I'm not so sure about that, Aunt Lucy, but thank you for saying it. I think we both know my pie baking skills wouldn't be something that would overly impress Father. He'd be more excited if he saw me marrying a wealthy businessman and living the life of a society woman in the city. An apple pie made in an old wooden stove in the middle of nowhere isn't quite up to those standards."

She laughed as her aunt gently tapped her on the arm and clucked her tongue. "Well, you're probably right, but if he could see how positively glowing you are since you've arrived out here, he wouldn't be able to see you living any other way. You look happier than I think I've ever seen you, even as a young girl. I do believe the fresh prairie air agrees with you, my dear."

For some reason, Kathryn's eyes wandered to where Colt walked with the children. He was between them, holding their hands until they spotted some of their friends over by the church and pulled free to go and play with them.

Colt was smiling widely, and her heart fluttered slightly at the sight. She was happy to see him so relaxed today, knowing how hard he worked every other day.

"So, are you feeling settled in at the Hammond's? Mr. Hammond is a good man, but I know sometimes he can be a bit rough around the edges, so I hope he's making you feel welcome. I mean, I've seen you at church and the few times you've come into town, so I would hope you'd tell me if you ever felt like you needed to come stay with me instead. I would always have a room for you."

Kathryn pulled her eyes away from Colt, who was now standing and talking with Old Tom.

"Everything's perfect, Aunt Lucy. You don't need to worry about me. Mrs. Hammond has been teaching me how to cook and bake, and Colt has been welcoming, even being willing to taste my cooking to help me improve. I know there've been a few times the food was barely edible, but he's never said anything unkind. I actually feel guilty sometimes knowing how hungry he had to be after working all day and having to eat food that I'm sure even the pigs on the farm would turn their snouts up at."

Her aunt laughed heartily and shook her head. "I'm sure you're exaggerating. By the look of these pies, I'd say you've come a long way then."

Kathryn shrugged nervously. She wasn't used to being praised, especially about anything even remotely domestic. And she knew she still had so much to learn. But it had been fun over the past few days when she would hurry up to the main house after school was let out to help with the evening meal. They'd had time during the weekends to even learn how to do some baking, which was something Kathryn had never believed she'd be able to do. Or, even enjoy.

However, she'd soon learned just how much she did enjoy it. The feeling of making something from scratch, all on her own, without needing anyone else to do it was unlike anything she'd ever experienced before. And then having that creation feed others, and hopefully someday, the people eating it would even look forward to her cooking.

She knew Colt had been polite more than he needed to be, even if there'd been a few times he couldn't hide his distaste. The family were used to eating Mrs. Hammond's delicious cooking, so it had been an adjustment to learn how to swallow hers most days.

The strange part was that she had Mrs. Hammond right beside her, guiding her and showing her what to do, so Kathryn couldn't quite figure out why the food didn't taste better when she was cooking it. Maybe some people just didn't have the ability, no matter how hard they tried.

She just hoped at least someone would bid on her pie, especially since the auction would be after the judging of the other pies they'd made and without much doubt, hers wouldn't be winning. It would be humiliating if no one even wanted hers at all.

After chatting with a few more of the townsfolk, she decided to wander around and take a look at all the booths set up around the middle of the town. Her eyes moved around, taking in the joy being radiated from every person she met.

This small town of Promise was unlike anything she'd ever experienced before. Everyone worked together, helped each other, and genuinely cared about their neighbors. Of course, there were a few people in the community who were less friendly, but for the most part, the entire town was filled with people who didn't have much for monetary value, but they made up for that in what truly mattered.

And this little fair, put together each year by everyone in the town, was a chance to just enjoy time together and celebrate the life they lived out here on the frontier.

"So, you must be the new schoolteacher everyone is talking about all over town. My name is Mrs. Martha Pembrooke. I run the Pembrooke school on the outskirts of town. How is the teaching going in that dilapidated old schoolhouse you've been assigned to?"

Kathryn offered a tense smile as the older woman approached her, standing in front of her so she had no choice but to stop and talk.

"Actually, the schoolhouse is wonderful. It has more than enough supplies for each of the students and it's been quite easy to get settled in."

"Well, you come from the city. I can't even fathom how they convinced you to settle for a teaching assignment like this, out here in the middle of nowhere. You would have had so much more opportunity if you'd stayed back east where the schools would have the best of everything. I'm sure they're not even able to pay you much."

"I was thrilled when my aunt contacted me to see if I'd be interested in teaching out here. The schools back east aren't any better than what I've found here."

Kathryn tried to keep her voice calm, but she could tell Mrs. Pembrooke was here to stir up trouble. A man stood beside her and he weakly tried to pull at her arm and keep her moving past.

But she wasn't budging.

"Oh, I don't believe that for a second. But now that you're here, I'd like to offer you the opportunity to teach at a real school, where you can make a difference with children who will actually be able to go far in life. And I'm certain the pay will be much more appealing than anything you're getting from the town for working in that public schoolhouse."

The plump woman was waving her hand around in disgust as she spoke about the little schoolhouse Kathryn taught at. A sudden urge hit her to defend the place she'd grown to love in the few short weeks she'd been here.

"I appreciate your offer, Mrs. Pembrooke, however I have to politely decline. You see, I'm here because I *do* want to make a difference in these children's lives. And just because the school I'm teaching in isn't as big or fancy as what you're providing, the students I have in my little school have just as much of a chance of going far in life as any others."

By now, she could feel herself starting to shake with anger, and she knew she needed to bring it under control before she made a scene. Already, a few people who had been nearby were stopping to listen to their conversation, knowing Mrs. Pembrooke wouldn't likely be making neighborly small talk with the new teacher in town.

Without thinking, her eyes automatically moved through the town center in search of Colt. He was standing next to the mercantile talking to

Caleb, but as though he could sense she was in need of help, his gaze found hers.

Mrs. Pembrooke turned her head to see what Kathryn was looking at, and when she looked back at her, one eyebrow was raised, and a smug smile took over her face.

"Well, I guess I can see why you're so loyal to your little school. I should have known. Surely you do remember that Mr. Hammond is a married man? It really doesn't look good for the new schoolteacher to be pining for a man who already has a wife."

Heat burned Kathryn's cheeks as she stared in shock at the woman in front of her. How dare she insinuate something so vile. Her stomach churned at the thought she'd ever given any hint of having feelings for Colt Hammond. Kathryn was willing to admit she was drawn to him, but she'd never given any indication of anything more than that. At least, she hadn't thought she had.

"Hi, Kathryn. I'm so glad to see you here. I was just talking to Mrs. Hammond and she showed me the pies you made. They look wonderful."

Kathryn slowly pulled her glare from Mrs. Pembrooke's and offered a weak smile to Mercy Brown as she came over and joined them.

"Hello, Mercy. I'm hopeful my pies might taste at least a little bit as good as they look." She tried to offer the other woman a joke, but she was still trying to calm her racing heart that was filled with anger at her conversation with the Pembrooke woman.

Mercy was eyeing them both carefully, looking back and forth with concern. Thankfully, she didn't say anything, but moved closer to Kathryn and gave her a genuine smile, reaching out and giving her hand a gentle squeeze before facing Mrs. Pembrooke.

"Constantine was looking for you and Uncle Clarence when we arrived. I think he went over by the feed mill if you want to go and find him," Mercy said guilelessly to Mrs. Pembrooke.

"Oh, thank you, Mercy. I hope you've been taking good care of him and not letting your expanding waistline stop you from helping around the farm. That boy works much too hard, so we do worry about him."

Mercy took a deep breath and held her smile. "I promise I'm still helping out as much as I can around the farm. You really don't need to worry about him."

The women stood and waited until the older

couple finally walked away. Kathryn worked to steady her racing heart before letting Mercy know how much she appreciated her coming over to help.

"Thanks for rescuing her, Mercy. I tried to get here as quick as I could, but it seemed like everyone wanted to suddenly stop and talk as I made my way over."

Kathryn jumped at the sound of Colt's voice from behind her. She turned, her hand fluttering up to her chest. "I didn't even hear you coming up."

He grinned and shrugged. "I really am starting to wonder if we do need to take you in to see about your hearing. You're much too easy to sneak up on."

"I hope Mrs. Pembrooke didn't say anything to upset you, Kathryn. I noticed you were looking a bit distressed when I walked over." Mercy was looking at her with concern.

Colt's smile dropped, and Kathryn immediately recognized the anger that filled his eyes. "What did she say to you, Kathryn?"

Not wanting to draw any more attention to them, or to ruin the fun of the day, Kathryn just waved her hand and laughed. "Honestly, I wasn't even paying attention. Something about her school being better than my school, or some silly notion. It's nothing to worry about."

She grabbed Mercy's hand and started to walk over to where some of the other women from town were visiting under a tree by the church as the children ran all around them. "Come on, we don't want to miss out on any of the exciting news the women will be sharing with each other."

She didn't let her eyes meet Colt's, but she could feel them boring holes into her back as she walked away. She just needed a few moments to gather herself and everything would be fine.

The last thing she needed was for Colt to find out exactly what Martha Pembrooke had said to her.

And how she'd suddenly realized how much of the woman's words might just have rung true.

CHAPTER 17

"Come on, Pa! It's almost time for the judging of the pies and then they'll have the auction. I sure do hope Miss Reeves isn't too upset if her pie doesn't win. I know she's been trying so hard to learn, but sometimes her food doesn't taste so good. I don't want to tell her, though, because I know it would hurt her feelings."

Colt smiled down at his daughter and reached out to ruffle her hair as she grabbed his hand and started pulling him toward the tables set up for the pies. "Oh, I don't think Miss Reeves will be too upset. She knows she still has a lot to learn, but it's good that you're minding your manners around her. It wouldn't be nice to make her feel bad when she's trying so hard to learn."

Delia stopped walking and looked up at him. "Remember when Ma was living with us? She never even tried to cook. How come she didn't want to learn too?"

Colt's heart stopped at the casual mention his daughter made about her ma and when she lived with them. She hadn't spoken much about it at all since the first few weeks of Arlene leaving, so he was caught off guard about the question.

"Well, I guess maybe your ma wasn't too interested in cooking, and since Grandma Winnie was still living there, it was just as easy for her to keep doing the cooking. But I'm sure your ma would have loved to learn someday."

How could he tell his daughter that her ma had made it very clear soon after they'd been married that cooking was not something she would be doing? Arlene had never wanted to learn, even when his own mother had offered many times to help teach her some simple recipes. She wanted nothing to do with any of the menial chores women living out here were expected to do.

Colt swallowed the familiar anger that started to bubble up in his throat. So many times over the past few years he'd sat and wondered how he could have possibly been so wrong about someone. He felt like a fool for being so taken in by her beauty that he hadn't been able to see through her false pretenses about wanting to be a perfect wife to him.

Now he knew the truth about who she was, and it killed him knowing he'd brought two children into the world who had to go through life without the love of a mother.

He didn't know if he'd ever be able to forgive himself for that.

And he vowed he'd never make that mistake again.

"What if she gets upset about not winning and decides to move away?"

Colt had to shake his head to get back to the conversation. It took him a few moments to realize Delia was back talking about Kathryn now, and not her mother.

He laughed and pulled at her hand to get her walking again. "Miss Reeves won't move away over losing a silly pie baking contest."

In fact, as much as he didn't like to admit he was wrong, Kathryn had shown a strength of character he'd never expected from her. He was starting to wonder if perhaps she might be able to handle living out here after all.

But it had still been less than a month, so he wasn't going to completely believe she could cope with frontier life just based on what he'd seen so far.

The heat had been relentless again today, and even though there was a light breeze, it did nothing to offer any relief. But the people of Promise didn't let it hamper their fun. Colt was sure he'd never seen so many people at their summer fair, but he figured since so many new settlers were coming to the area every year, it made sense. He remembered coming to the fairs as a child and now as he watched his son playing a game of ball over by the mercantile, his heart filled with happiness knowing his own children could experience life in this little town.

They'd all enjoyed lunch scattered around the town, everyone laying out blankets to enjoy their picnics they'd packed, each family trying to find a little spot of shade to rest from the heat. Kathryn seemed to be having fun and had shared a conversation with both Fae and Caleb who'd joined their family to eat.

But he knew she was still holding something back about that conversation with Martha

Pembrooke, and he intended to find out what had upset her.

Now, his eyes moved to where she stood by the table with the other women who'd entered pies to be judged. Each of the pies had only been given a number so none of the judges could be biased about the pie they were tasting. Old Tom, Doc Jacobs, Caleb, and a few other men from the town had been chosen to taste each of the pies and then decide among themselves which one deserved the ribbon.

Kathryn looked nervous as they made their way toward one of the pies, and he knew immediately it had to be hers. He held his breath, hoping the men would at least be kind enough not to make any faces as they took a bite.

Thankfully, each of them ate without giving anything away and moved on to the next pie. He watched as she visibly relaxed too. For a woman who had grown up in the city and had never needed to do anything for herself, it still amazed him how these simple little things like making a pie for a small town fair could mean so much to her.

As he stood beside his daughter, watching this woman beaming with pride and excitement over something he would have never thought she'd care about, he realized there was a lot more to Kathryn Reeves than even he might have been willing to admit.

KATHRYN SAT under one of the trees along the edge of the church yard, vaguely listening to the other women talking. She sipped on a lemonade and sighed with relief as the cold liquid made its way down her throat.

The wind had picked up during the day, as she was becoming accustomed to out here, but as she'd soon discovered, quite often even the winds didn't bring any relief from the heat. If anything, it seemed to just move the hotness around more.

But even with the uncomfortable warmth, Kathryn couldn't remember a day in her life when she'd had more fun.

After her earlier run-in with Martha Pembrooke, she'd been sure the day would be ruined. However, the town of Promise had lived up to its name today and made sure that every resident here had the best time possible.

Spirits were high, laughter was plentiful, and

friendships were cherished throughout the day. For the first time in her life, Kathryn truly felt like she belonged.

She knew it would sound so strange to anyone who'd grown up with less than her to be able to understand how she could feel that way. It wasn't like her family hadn't been wonderful—in fact, Kathryn knew she'd been truly blessed to have the life she'd been given.

But it hadn't changed the fact she'd never liked living in the city. The way they'd lived hadn't been her choice, and so many times she'd found herself simply going through the motions of what she was expected to be doing. It was never the life she would have chosen for herself.

Kathryn preferred the quiet life she had found out here. The kind of place where the work was harder, but the reward was sweeter. She was witness to it every day as neighbors helped neighbors without question and everyone enjoyed the simpler things life had to offer. It wasn't about material goods or monetary value.

What mattered to the people here was family, friendship, and community. As long as they had enough to survive, they would give their last dime to help one another.

Her eyes found the familiar figure of the man who'd undoubtedly become someone she knew she could count on. Even though he'd irritated her and seemed a bit gruff from time to time, Colt was someone she could trust.

"I still can't believe your pie went for such a high price. Colt must really enjoy your baking for him to pay that much for it."

Fae's voice pulled her back into the conversation as she turned her gaze to her friend's smiling face. "Well, I don't know about that, because truthfully, there have been many evenings the past week I know he was having trouble swallowing the ones I made. I think he and Caleb were just trying to be nice."

Mercy laughed as she adjusted her legs under herself to get more comfortable on the blanket. "It was quite entertaining to watch the two of them bidding. They're good men and they were determined to make sure your pie got the best price."

Now Kathryn laughed and rolled her eyes. "It went for even more than Mrs. Pembrooke's, and she won the pie contest judging. She didn't look happy when my pie got the highest bid."

"I imagine poor old Uncle Clarence got an earful for missing the auction. He could have at least kept the bidding going. I had visions of her pulling him by the ear back home when she went stomping away to find him." Mercy tried to look serious, but soon all three women were giggling like schoolgirls, trying not to be too loud in case anyone overheard them.

"Miss Reeves! Hurry, I need you to be my partner for the three-legged race. Owen is going with Pa, and I really want to beat him." Delia ran over and grabbed her by the arm, trying to pull her up from the ground.

Kathryn quickly jumped up to join the child, not even sure what exactly a three-legged race would be. She let Delia drag her over to the mercantile where a large crowd of people had gathered for the races. Most of the participants were children, with some parents joining as partners.

"Miss Reeves is my partner. We're going to win!"

Colt was crouched down beside Owen, tying a piece of rope around their legs, joining them together. A wide grin spread across his face as he stood up and leaned his arm on Owen's shoulders.

"Is that right? Miss Reeves, have you ever taken part in a three-legged race before? I mean, it does take some fancy footwork and a bit of skill to get to the finish line. And from what I've seen in the short time I've known you, I'm not too sure if this is a good idea."

Kathryn pretended to scowl but knew her smile gave her away. He was trying to ruffle her feathers by mentioning her few "mishaps" where she might not have been as graceful as other women.

But she was determined not to let him get to her. "Just tell me what to do and be prepared to lose."

He laughed and shook his head, then bent down to pick up a piece of rope beside him. "Tie this around your inside legs to join you together. Then, you need to make it to the finish line tied together without falling over."

"Sounds simple enough." She bent down and tied her leg to Delia's, who was beaming with excitement.

"Miss Reeves, we just need to get a good rhythm going. But remember my legs aren't as long as yours." As the child tried to explain the best way they could make it to the finish line first, Kathryn turned and caught Colt smiling smugly.

She looked down at Owen and offered her hand to him.

"Good luck, Owen."

The boy looked just as excited as his father when the racers were told to all take their marks. When Reverend Moore hollered go, Kathryn quickly tried to take off, but soon realized this was not going to be as easy as she'd hoped.

Her arm was around Delia's shoulders as the girl struggled to hold onto her waist. Already, Owen and Colt were slightly ahead, and Delia was laughing excitedly, telling her to hurry so they could catch them. It was as though there weren't any other racers as the four of them competed to beat the other.

Just as she was sure they'd finally figured out a good rhythm, Delia tripped slightly and they both ended up falling to the ground in a cloud of dust. But as they fell, she saw that Colt and Owen had fallen too, so they still had a chance.

She was sure by now she was covered in dirt and her hair was likely hanging completely loose down her back, but she quickly stood up and got Delia righted beside her. They were both laughing so hard it was difficult to catch their breath.

"Miss Reeves! We have to hurry!"

They made their way to the finish line just as Colt and Owen managed to get back up and race alongside them. People were cheering all around them, but all she could hear was the laughter coming from Owen and Delia. To see these children having so much fun warmed her heart.

With one final push, she sprinted forward, dragging Delia with her. They fell over the finish line in another cloud of dust and laughter at the same time Colt and Owen were landing in a heap beside them.

"Oh, what a close finish. What do you say, folks? Do we have a winner, or was it a tie?" The reverend was clapping with excitement as he looked around at the spectators.

The crowd cheered as Kathryn stood back up, bringing Delia with her, and dusted off her skirts. Delia was already trying to jump up and down with excitement, almost knocking Kathryn back over.

"We beat you! The girls won!"

"No way! We beat you! The boys won!"

The kids were arguing good-naturedly while they waited to see who would be declared the winner. Kathryn was trying to untie the rope from their feet before Delia dragged her over, and when she finally succeeded, she stood up, her eyes slamming into Colt's.

He'd been laughing with the children, insisting that the boys had won, until their eyes met. As soon as they did, the smile fell from his face like he'd seen a ghost and he turned away.

Her own smile faded slowly as she tried to figure out what had happened to make him suddenly angry with her. There was no other way to explain the look on his face.

How could a day that had been almost perfect, giving her a sense of home and joy she'd never imagined possible, fall apart so quickly with one simple glance?

CHAPTER 18

Colt knew he needed to apologize to Kathryn for his sour mood on the way home from the fair. But how could he apologize for something he didn't even understand himself?

Everything had been perfect through the day, other than the run-in she'd had with Mrs. Pembrooke, and he knew Kathryn and the kids had all been having a wonderful time. He'd ended up paying more for her pie than he should have but seeing the joy on her face had been worth every penny.

Then, they'd joined the three-legged race and he couldn't remember the last time he'd laughed as much as he did watching Kathryn and Delia make their way toward the finish line. With everyone

147

falling over and the cheering from the crowd, he'd almost let himself believe for a moment he was living a normal life with a wife and children.

Except, when their eyes had met, he'd been hit with the realization that she *wasn't* his wife, and nothing he was feeling had been real.

And he'd been struck with a pain so hard in his chest, it had taken his breath away. His children had been enjoying the day just as much as he had, and he knew he couldn't let them fall into that false reality too.

So, as soon as the tie had been declared, and they'd received their ribbons, he'd quickly gathered up his mother and told the family they were going home.

He knew he'd been surly and had practically dragged them all to the wagon, then barely spoken a word all the way home. And when he'd helped Kathryn down from the wagon, he'd been sure not to hold onto her hand for too long.

She'd politely declined the offer to stay for supper at the house and held her head up as she walked to her cabin, seeming to instinctively know he was angry about something, but not knowing why. His mother had been scolding him, but he'd barely heard a word as he'd watched Kathryn disappear into the distance.

Now he stood on the front porch, unable to keep his gaze from moving toward the little cabin nestled back among the trees. The sun was just making its way beneath the horizon, leaving a trail of orange, purple, and red filling the sky for as far as his eyes could see.

Everything around him seemed still as he listened to the birds singing their nightly songs. He slapped at the bug that was biting his neck and leaned against the post by the steps, breathing deeply of the fresh evening air as he tried to make sense of his thoughts.

While he watched the cabin, he noticed movement outside the door, and his breath caught when he recognized the figure of the woman he'd been thinking about. She came out and stood next to her own front door, looking out across the fields.

Even from this distance, Colt knew she was beautiful.

Before he knew what was happening, his feet were moving down the path toward her cabin. The sky was starting to get dark now, and while it wasn't proper to go to a single woman's home at this time of night, he needed to see her and apologize for how he'd acted earlier.

"You shouldn't be standing outside in the dark on your own." As soon as he said the words, he cringed. It wasn't exactly the nice apology he'd planned when he saw her.

Kathryn jumped and turned to face him, her hand flying up to her chest in fright. Her hair hung down around her shoulders, framing her face in the glow from the lamp she'd hung out by the door. She wore a long white nightgown, and he knew if he were any kind of gentleman, he'd turn around and not cause her any more embarrassment.

"Colt! What are you doing here?" She looked around with a panicked expression before reaching back inside the door and pulling a shawl off the hook to wrap around herself.

"Well, I came down with the intention of apologizing for my earlier mood, but now I guess I've got to apologize for startling you, and also for still standing here while you're in your nightclothes. My mom would be dragging me home by my ear if she knew I'd come down here and intruded on you at this time of night."

He offered her a smile, hoping she would be

forgiving. And as he'd expected of her, she laughed softly and shook her head. "It's all right, you just startled me. This is the first night I was feeling brave enough to come outside as it grew dark, but I was hoping for some cool air to help me get to sleep. I'm always afraid of the coyotes who I'm pretty sure surround my cabin every night, waiting for me to come outside."

He moved over and stood by her, turning to face the same direction as her so he wouldn't be staring at her in her nightgown. Even completely covered with her shawl, which had to be causing her discomfort from the already too hot air around them, he was having a hard time concentrating on what she was saying.

"Well, normally the coyotes won't bother you too much, unless they're sick or hungry. But I wouldn't suggest being outside on your own in the dark, if you can help it."

Why was he standing here talking about the threat of coyotes, instead of just saying his apology and getting back up to his own house? He knew he shouldn't be here, but he couldn't make himself leave now that he was.

They stood in an awkward silence, both looking out to the now dark sky. In the distance, frogs croaked loudly down by the creek and as they watched, the horizon in the distance lit up with pink that spread across the sky.

"Looks like we're going to get a storm."

He rolled his eyes at his own comment. Kathryn was a smart woman. She would have been able to figure out by seeing the lightning, there was a good chance of a storm.

Colt felt like he was a schoolboy trying to woo the cute girl who sat in front of him in class but being too awkward to know what to say.

"So, I did come down to apologize for being so grumpy today on the way home from the fair. I hope I didn't ruin your day too much." He glanced over at her and offered a smile. "But for supper, I had a piece of your pie which I paid so handsomely for, and it was actually quite delicious. You've come a long way in the past couple of weeks."

She smiled and looked back out at the sky. He wondered if she was nervous about the impending storm. They hadn't had much rain or storms since she'd arrived, so it was possible she was concerned about being down here on her own.

"Well, I did worry that perhaps I'd done something to upset you. I thought we'd all been having a good day, and then it seemed like I'd made you angry."

If he hadn't felt bad already, he would have after hearing the confusion in her voice. He'd ruined a day that should have been a happy memory for her.

He knew he owed her an explanation, but he wasn't sure where to start. Quickly thrusting his hands through his hair, he took a deep breath and leaned back against the wall.

"I've mentioned before that I'm not much of a gentleman, but I guess I can't use that as an excuse every time I do something wrong. And to be completely honest, since the day you arrived in town, I feel like I've been saying and doing all the wrong things."

He met her eyes and smiled apologetically.

Her brows furrowed as she waited for him to continue.

"But today, when I let myself have fun, and then saw how much fun the children were having, everything just hit me about what they're missing in their lives. And no matter how much I might want to pretend otherwise, we don't have a regular family who can be out enjoying days like today." He swallowed hard and cleared his throat.

"I just can't let the children get used to having fun like this, knowing how hard it will be for them when you leave. They can't start believing everything will always be like this when it won't."

The silence was deafening, and he was sure even the frogs had stopped their singing as they waited to hear what Kathryn was going to say.

"Colt Hammond, I've put up with you causing me to fall out of a wagon, tumble head over heels into the creek, and many other infuriating moments since the day I arrived in town. But never, have I been more angry than I am now. You've never believed, not once, that I was going to make it out here. You keep thinking I'm leaving and that I'm not cut out for life on the frontier."

He opened his mouth to try and interrupt so he could explain himself, but her face was red, and her eyes glowed with anger as she stepped a little closer. Her hands were clenched in fists at her side, holding onto the edges of her shawl, no longer even trying to cover her nightgown.

"Well, I've got news for you. I don't know what happened with her, but I think it's about time you realized, I'm not your wife. Just because one woman you knew didn't stay here, doesn't mean every other woman is going to do the same. And it's not fair for you to keep saying it."

If she'd punched him in the stomach, it wouldn't have been any more of a shock.

But he knew with every angry word she uttered; she was speaking the truth.

CHAPTER 19

Kathryn ground her teeth together to keep from saying anything more. She knew she wasn't behaving very ladylike, but right now, she didn't care.

She was tired.

She was tired of having to try so hard all the time to prove herself to everyone. And ever since the day she'd arrived in Promise, Colt had made it clear he didn't think she could handle it and would be running back home at the first inconvenience.

The part that made her even more angry, was the fact that she even cared so much what this man thought of her.

She pulled her shawl back up tightly around her shoulders and looked out to the sky once more as she tried to calm her shaking. Another flash of lightning lit up the horizon, but thankfully it was still a long way off, so hopefully she would be asleep before the storm reached them.

Colt remained silent, and she had a moment of regret for what she'd said. She knew she shouldn't have brought his wife up, but she'd just been so wild and the words tumbled from her mouth without thinking.

"When Arlene left, I had the job of trying to explain to my children why their mother had chosen to leave her family behind. I guess the anger and bitterness I've held in over the past few months has just left me unable to believe that any woman who wasn't raised out here would want to live here. Or that they could cope with the life that is so different from city life."

This was the first time he'd really opened up about his wife, so she didn't dare interrupt now that he was talking. She waited patiently for him to find the words to explain it.

"She hated it here. I met her when I went out east for a few weeks with my mother to visit family. My pa had died a couple of years before, so I didn't like her going off on her own. We went after harvest was done, and my younger brother stayed back to look after the livestock."

He shook his head as he laughed bitterly. "I was a young, country hayseed who'd never been outside of Promise. When I met Arlene, I'd never seen a woman so sophisticated, and I didn't stand a chance. She was going through a rebellious phase with her wealthy parents and wanted to punish them.

"I know now that's all it was, but I was naive, and after spending two weeks with her, I thought I was in love. I convinced her to marry me, and for some reason, she believed I was like the wealthy farmers who lived around the city where she'd grown up. She was excited for some grand adventure out in the country." He stopped and shook his head, laughing bitterly. "My mother was so angry with me, but I wasn't thinking straight, and I thought this fancy city woman was truly in love with me too."

Kathryn suddenly felt guilty that Colt thought he needed to explain this all to her. She knew how hard it had to be.

"I'm sure she must have been in love with you, at least a bit, to agree to marry you and move out here." She hated to think the woman had never had any feelings for the man she married.

He laughed harshly. "Oh, I think she thought she was, in the beginning. It was a whirlwind. She'd shown her parents they couldn't control her, and she was the first of her friends to be married. She thought it was quite exciting." He leaned forward, resting his elbows on the railing by the step. "That is, until we arrived home and she saw where she'd be living."

"But it's so beautiful here, surely she must have been excited to start her new life." Kathryn couldn't imagine feeling any other way about this little community.

"We tried to make it work, but she never had any interest in learning how to live out here. Shortly after the twins were born, she almost convinced me to move back to Chicago and give up my life here. By then, her parents had pretty much disowned her, so she was stuck with me because there was no way she could take care of herself without her father's money."

"Oh, Colt. You would have been miserable. I can't imagine you living anywhere but here on your farm."

He glanced over at her and smiled. "I would

have been, but truthfully, I didn't know what else to do. She was angry all the time, she had barely any interest in the children, and even told me one time during one of her many tirades how furious she was to be tied here now because of them."

Kathryn gasped softly and shook her head sadly. "Surely she didn't mean it." The words were spoken so quietly, she wasn't sure if he'd even heard her.

He shrugged. "I don't know. All I do know is that she became more and more miserable, until the day the traveling theater came to town. I thought it would be something that would excite her and couldn't wait to take her to a show."

Kathryn's heart sunk as she realized what he was about to say.

"They stayed in town for a week, putting on shows every evening for people from all of the surrounding communities to come and watch. Arlene made friends with one of the women in the show and would go into town during the day to spend time learning everything behind the scenes. By the time they were set to leave, she came and told me she was going with them, believing she'd found something that could truly make her happy. She told me she would never have that as long as she was stuck on this farm, with children she'd never wanted, and a husband she didn't love."

Thunder rumbled quietly in the distance, the only sound between them as Kathryn moved closer to Colt, unsure how to offer him the comfort he needed.

"I know it's hard to understand why things happen the way they do sometimes, but you always have to believe there is a reason. Even though things might not have worked out for you and your wife, at least you have Delia and Owen. If not for her, you wouldn't have the wonderful children you've been blessed with."

He smiled sadly and nodded. "I thank God every day for those children. But I also worry because I know I can't give them what a mother can. They deserve better than what they've gotten. They're always going to be those children whose mother chose to leave them." His jaw moved like he was holding his anger back. "And I'm the man who couldn't give his wife enough to make her want to stay here."

"Colt, it's not your fault Arlene couldn't see what she had here. She had a beautiful home, children who loved her, and a husband who tried everything to make her happy. You can't blame yourself for the problems that were within her. If she couldn't appreciate everything she had, then you're far better off without her."

His eyes lifted to hers, and she realized she was now standing so close to him she could hear every breath he took. Suddenly, she had a question she needed to hear the answer to.

"Do you still love her?"

The words were whispered, and her heart pounded so hard in her chest, she was afraid she wouldn't hear the answer.

How could she have asked him such a personal question? And why did she care so much?

He kept his eyes on hers and slowly shook his head. "I worry every day that I'll never be able to love a woman again. And if I do, she won't be able to love me, or be happy with what I have to offer."

She swallowed, unable to speak as his breath touched her face. Without noticing, he'd brought his head closer to hers, and before she knew what was happening, his lips were on hers.

Even as her mind was yelling for her to stop, knowing this wasn't appropriate behavior for a single schoolteacher, her body rebelled and moved closer. When his hand gently reached up and cupped her cheek, while his other arm wound behind her back and pulled her against him, she knew nothing her mind said would convince her to pull away.

His lips moved while his fingers moved up into her hair at the base of her neck, slowly caressing the skin and leaving a trail of heat everywhere he touched.

He groaned low in his throat, while he kissed her with an urgency that left her breathless. Just when she thought her legs were about to give out, he pulled his head back and looked down at her. Her lips were still parted, and it took her a moment to get her senses back.

"I'm sorry. I shouldn't have done that."

His voice sounded hoarse as he struggled against the emotions of what had just happened.

Suddenly, he turned his head and his eyebrows pulled together. "Can you smell smoke?"

She shook her head, trying to get rid of the cobwebs as she struggled to comprehend what he was saying.

He stepped back, and walked down the step, sniffing in the air loudly.

"Something's burning."

The scent of smoke finally reached her, and she

stepped down beside him. "I can smell it. Where is it coming from?"

He turned and scanned the area, stopping as he faced the trees separating the property in the distance from Constantine and Mercy Brown's.

The sky just above the tree line was orange, and with a sudden realization of what was happening, Colt took off running.

Kathryn didn't know if she could keep up, but she wasn't going to be left behind.

As they raced through the long grass toward the smoke she could now make out billowing high in the air, she sent up a prayer for her friend and her unborn child.

"Please, let Mercy be all right."

CHAPTER 20

As soon as he made it across the field separating his property from Brown's, Colt knew from the location of the flames that it was the barn on fire. With the lack of rain they'd had, he also knew that everything around the area was now at risk too.

He ran straight toward the fire, not even sure what he was going to do, but the sound of Mercy's screams coming from just outside the doorway terrified him.

When he got closer, he could see her trying to get inside, screaming her husband's name.

"Mercy, get back! Go up to the house." He turned and saw Kathryn not too far behind him, so he pushed Mercy toward her. "Take her to the house."

"Constantine is inside. I tried to get in, but the flames are so high…"

"Come on, Mercy. Colt will take care of everything here. Let's go."

Colt knew Kathryn would look after Mercy, so he turned his attention to the barn. He knew there was no way he could get this under control on his own, but he had to try.

And as much as he hated Constantine Brown, if the man was inside the burning barn, Colt had to try and save him. He looked around and saw a large pail by the pump, so he raced over and started filling it with water. Even knowing it wasn't going to make much difference, he hoped it would at least give him something to use as he made his way inside.

Pounding hoofbeats came from the other side of the house and another neighbor hollered to him.

"I'm going to go in and get some men from town."

"Constantine is inside."

The other man cursed as he tried to keep his

horse under control. "Wait until I get back with some help. Don't be going in on your own."

As the neighbor raced off toward town, Colt ran back to the barn with the full pail of water, almost running straight into Kathryn who was heading the other way with an empty pail.

"What are you doing out here? I told you to take Mercy to the house and look after her."

"She's inside, but I need to help you. She promised to stay in the house."

Colt didn't have time to argue with the woman right now, so he just shook his head and continued to the fire that now had the entire building engulfed in flames.

He threw the bucket of water at the open doorway then turned and almost knocked Kathryn over. "Here, take this one too." He grabbed it from her and tossed it on the fire.

The water eased some of the flames near the doorway, so he ran toward it, putting his arm up to shield his eyes from the sparks.

"Colt, no! Don't go in there!"

Kathryn was screaming from behind him and he could make out the fear in her voice, but he needed to get inside now while he still could. He quickly pulled his collar up and tucked his face down enough to keep the smoke out a bit.

His skin burned as the heat of the flames licked at him, and he had to leap over a burning board that had fallen to the floor. He squinted his eyes as he scanned the area to see if he could find Constantine. Even though he'd covered his face, his lungs heaved as he struggled to breathe.

Finally, in the far corner, he could make out the figure of the man slouched on the floor. He dodged falling debris and sparks as he made his way over to him.

Constantine was unconscious, so he just grabbed him and lifted him up over his shoulder. It would have been easier to drag the man, but there were too many burning boards to get over before they made it back outside.

Every breath he took hurt, and Colt started to think he wasn't going to make it back to the open doorway where Kathryn stood throwing another bucket of water at the fire. He had a moment of guilt knowing if he didn't make it out of here, that he hadn't let her know how much he cared about her.

When she finally saw him coming back through

the flames, she dropped the pail and started to step inside, reaching out for him.

"Get back." His voice was hoarse, but knowing she was about to put herself at risk gave him the final bit of strength he needed to get out before she was hurt.

He came outside and gulped for air as he took a few more steps to get far enough away before dropping the man to the ground. Colt fell down beside him on his hands and knees, coughing violently as he tried to get the fresh air into his lungs he so desperately needed.

Kathryn kneeled on the ground beside him. "Colt, are you all right?" Her voice was loud even with the noise of the burning building behind them.

"I'm fine. But, I'm not so sure about him."

He lifted his head and looked at Kathryn, who was already leaning over the other man to listen for his breathing.

"Constantine!"

Colt closed his eyes as he heard Mercy's anguished cry behind him. As the woman dropped to the ground beside them, she glanced at Kathryn. "Is he...?"

Kathryn looked at Colt, and he knew without

her saying a word that Constantine Brown was dead.

And the sobbing that filled the air just as the sounds of hoofbeats indicated more help had arrived, told Colt that Mercy knew too.

KATHRYN WATCHED out the window as the skies finally opened and threw down the rain. A crack of thunder startled her just as the sky lit up, illuminating the figures of the men who'd been working tirelessly for the past hour to keep the fire contained to the barn and not spread farther. She had just about given up hope that they would ever get the fire out, so thankfully, her prayers had been answered.

She walked over to the door of the bedroom where poor Mercy was finally getting some sleep. Thankfully, Doc Jacobs had shown up to fight the fire and had some medicine to help the new widow get some rest.

She peeked in to make sure her friend hadn't been woken up by the thunder, then pulled the door closed, knowing the men would be coming inside once the fire was completely out. As long as the rain kept up for a while, hopefully the last of the embers would be doused and nothing else would be lost.

The past couple of hours were a blur in her mind as she finally sat down in the rocking chair by the window. Even though Kathryn had only met Constantine a few times, and didn't really know him well, her heart ached for her friend.

She'd heard a few things from Colt and some others in town over the weeks, that gave her reason to believe Constantine might not have been a good man, especially when it came to his treatment of his wife. But she also knew the grief her friend was feeling was real. Not only had she lost her husband, she was left with a baby on the way, and a future she wasn't sure of anymore.

Kathryn's heart ached for the pain and hardship she knew Mercy was now going to be faced with in the months ahead.

As another flash of lightning lit up the sky, her eyes found Colt's familiar figure among the other men around the barn. The rain was still coming down, leaving a pile of charred rubble and gray ashes on the ground where the fire had once raged. There were still areas with small flames under some of the boards, but within a few more minutes of rain, everything would be put out.

She got up to put some water in the kettle to make the men something warm now they'd be soaked through to the skin. She was still in her nightgown, but Mercy had offered her a tattered dressing gown, so she could cover herself up before any of the men could see her.

Of course, Colt had already seen her that way, but for some reason, it didn't really bother Kathryn as much as it should. In her heart, she knew she could trust him to not take advantage of her, and he would never make her feel like she'd been improper.

Her cheeks warmed as she remembered their kiss. Even just thinking about it made her heart skip a beat. But as soon as the feeling had hit her, she was slammed with the reality that she'd kissed a married man.

How would she ever be able to look him in the eye again?

She jumped as the door opened, and she dropped the kettle onto the wood stove with a bang. Colt walked through, water dripping from his shoulders, and right behind him were Caleb,

Doc Jacobs, and a couple of other men who'd been helping.

"The fire's pretty much out now, so the rest of the men have headed back home. I'm going to stay here for a bit longer and make sure the embers don't flare up if you want to get Doc here to take you home."

Kathryn shook her head and pulled the dressing gown tighter around her. "No, I'm going to stay here with Mercy until she wakes up. I don't want her to be alone."

Caleb nodded as he walked over and grabbed a towel from beside the washing bowl, then started to dry his neck. "That's likely a good idea. I'll get Fae to come here first thing to take over sitting with her so you can get home."

Just then, the door slammed open, and Mrs. Pembrooke burst inside. "I just heard all the ruckus around town about the fire out here. Where is my nephew? Where is Constantine?"

She was disheveled and soaking wet from her ride out to the farm as she looked around frantically at the people inside the house. Her normally perfectly coiffed hair hung limply beneath her sleeping bonnet, and the coat she'd thrown over her nightdress had been hastily tied with one side higher than the other.

Doc Jacobs went over and put his hands comfortingly on her shoulders. "I'm sorry to tell you, Mrs. Pembrooke, but Constantine was inside the barn when it caught fire. He didn't make it out."

She glared at them one by one. "Why didn't you save him? What were you all doing?"

"Mrs. Pembrooke, Colt was the first one here, and he did go in and try saving him, but it was too late."

But she wasn't listening to any of them. It looked like rage was now fueled by her grief, and she didn't want to hear anything they said. She walked over to Colt, her eyebrows pulled together in anger, pointing her finger at his chest.

"You did this. You never liked my Constantine, and you were always trying to take his land. I heard you even fought with him a couple of weeks ago in town, right in front of everyone. It seems very suspicious to me that you were the first one to arrive. How do we know you didn't set the fire on purpose to get rid of him?"

"Mrs. Pembrooke! You can't be accusing people of things like that, especially ones who have just spent the best part of the night outside fighting the fire. And, risking their own lives." Poor Doc Jacobs was trying to calm her down, but she was too angry.

"And where is my nephew's no-good wife? Maybe she was involved too."

Kathryn walked over, holding her hands in fists by her side, no longer willing to stand back and let this woman speak like this. "Mercy is finally asleep, and if you think she could have ever done anything like this, then you can turn around and leave this instant. I don't need her to wake up and hear any of your hatred being spewed."

"I'm not leaving until I know what happened." She turned back to Colt. "I'm going to make sure you're arrested for this. I know you had your hand in it. Just because your family was one of the founding settlers of this community, doesn't mean we can turn a blind eye to what you've done. Constantine told me how much you harassed him."

Colt had been quietly leaning against the rickety table that looked like it would fall apart at any moment, with his arms crossed over his chest. The only thing that gave away his own anger was the flash in his eyes as he listened to the woman ramble.

"I never burned anything down, so you go ahead and tell anyone you want. No one will believe you. I have my own land, and my own barn. The last thing I needed was anything from Constantine."

"Oh, I promise you, by the time I'm finished, everyone will believe me. I'll find the proof I need. Since you were the first one here, I believe you were already here when it started. *Because you were the one who set it.*"

Kathryn stepped forward, unwilling to let Colt be blamed for something he had nothing to do with. He caught her eyes with his and gave a subtle shake of his head, telling her without words to step back.

"Well, Sheriff Harkins is due in town tomorrow. So, we'll let him settle this. I'm not going to let you get away with this." With those words hanging in the air, the plump woman turned and walked out the door.

Kathryn turned to look at the men who'd been left watching in shock. "What's going to happen?" She was terrified to hear the answer. Mrs. Pembrooke didn't seem like the kind of person you wanted to trifle with.

Colt just shrugged and pushed himself up.

"She's just riled up. By morning, she'll calm down and see reason. If you're going to stay here with Mercy, we'll all get going so you can try to get some sleep too."

But as the men walked out the door, just as the rain was letting up and leaving her with the smell of smoke all around her, Kathryn knew she wouldn't be getting any sleep.

And even though Colt was determined to keep her from telling the truth about where he was when the fire started, Kathryn knew if Mrs. Pembrooke wasn't going to let this go, she must say something to clear his name.

Even if it meant smearing her own.

CHAPTER 21

*C*olt leaned against the rail on the steps as he watched the procession come up the road toward the house. Dust hung in the air already, even after the rain last night. The ground had been so dry, whatever moisture had accumulated was quickly soaked into the dirt.

He recognized the buggy belonging to the Pembrooke's, and he knew the horse riding alongside would be Sheriff Harkins. As acting sheriff in this area, he rode from town to town, spending time wherever he was needed. But, with the amount of settlers flooding the area, it was just a matter of time before Promise needed to have their own full-time sheriff on hand to keep the peace.

Colt wasn't really worried about what would happen, because he knew Mrs. Pembrooke didn't have any kind of evidence. She was all fired up right now, and likely Sheriff Harkins knew he just needed to appease the woman so she would give it up.

Thankfully, Colt had known Jackson Harkins for a while now and they had a good friendship. Colt had even helped a few times with tracking and escorting prisoners when needed. So, he knew whatever happened, Jackson would be fair and wouldn't just listen to the words of a woman who was clearly off her rocker.

His mother came out and stood on the step beside him with her hands on her hips. He was glad the children were both playing down by the creek, enjoying the unexpected day off from school after Kathryn had been up all night with Mercy.

"This woman isn't going to let this go, is she? I swear, every day she gets a little bit more ornery and unbearable. Since the day we mentioned opening our school back up, she's had a bee in her bonnet and just can't be satisfied until she gets it closed back down so hers is the only school in the district."

"She can accuse me all she wants, but she's got no proof to back her words."

His mother now wiped her hands on her apron nervously. "I don't know, Colt. The Pembrookes have a lot of money and sometimes, that's enough to swing people to their way of thinking."

As they pulled into the yard, Colt was glad to see Caleb had ridden out with them. At least he would have another ally beside him.

Jackson tipped the front of his hat in greeting as they stopped in front of the steps. "Colt. Good to see you."

"Enough with the niceties. Do what you've been told to do out here." Mrs. Pembrooke was already scrambling out of her buggy in a massive explosion of silks and ruffled skirts. "This man had every reason to want to be rid of Constantine, and I expect you to do your job and find out the truth."

Jackson held his gaze steady on the older woman, but Colt could see his jaw twitch as he fought to control his annoyance with her. "Mrs. Pembrooke, I assure you, I know my job. And, I also know that no matter how much you shout at me or anyone else, it's not going to make me do anything different. Now, if you'll just stand over there quietly, I will talk to Colt and see what he says happened."

Colt couldn't hold back the smile as he watched Mrs. Pembrooke's mouth open, then close as Jackson stared her down. The sheriff was a fair man, but he also wasn't someone you wanted to argue with. He dismounted, then walked over to the steps where Colt stood. "Mrs. Pembrooke has some accusations about the fire last night at Constantine Brown's. Can you give me your version of what happened?"

"Not much to tell you, other than I smelled smoke so I ran through the field dividing our property to see what it was. By the time I got there, the barn was engulfed in flames. Mrs. Brown was outside, and she told me her husband was inside the barn, so I went in to get him. When I carried him out, he was already dead."

Mrs. Pembrooke gasped, and Colt felt a moment of guilt for being so blunt about her nephew's condition. But he was also getting annoyed at having to explain himself after he could have been killed too.

"So, you were at home when the fire started?"

Colt swallowed as he nodded, not wanting to

lie but he figured he was at home since he was on his property.

"Don't believe him. He's been wanting to get that bit of land along the trees for years, and Constantine told me he threatened him numerous times. He wanted to get rid of him so he could keep plowing more and more of it for himself."

Colt took a deep breath to keep his anger under control. "That land you're referring to is already mine, and it always has been. It was your nephew who couldn't seem to understand that fact. So, you're crazy if you think I needed to *get rid of anybody* to plow my own land."

Jackson was obviously just as annoyed as Colt, as he pushed his hands through his hair in frustration before turning to face Martha again. "Mrs. Pembrooke, I've already asked you once to stay quiet while I ask the questions. If you keep interrupting, I'm leaving." He faced his mother and smiled. "Mrs. Hammond, can you verify that your son was at home last night around the time the fire started?"

She swallowed hard and glanced at Colt with a panicked look. He knew his God-fearing mother would never be able to lie. "Well, he was here. He had stepped outside for some fresh air just around dusk and then went for a walk, from what I know."

"I told you! He wasn't even in the house. He was at Constantine's setting the fire, then he pretended he was the hero rushing in to save the day, knowing full well he would be too late."

She was giddy with excitement now that she thought she'd figured out her accusations had just been proven true. Jackson looked pained, knowing full well Colt's mother had just left room for doubt about his whereabouts. Even though Colt was sure the sheriff believed he was innocent, he was going to have to do his job and make sure he found out the truth.

"No, he wasn't at Constantine's. He was with me. Down at my cabin by the schoolhouse."

In all the commotion, Colt hadn't even noticed Kathryn walking up toward the house until they heard her voice. He cringed, knowing she had just destroyed her own reputation by admitting he was down with her.

"Excuse me, Miss? Who are you?" Jackson turned to see who had just spoken, obviously confused at this turn of events.

Mrs. Pembrooke stepped forward, her face red with anger. "She's the new schoolteacher in town.

The *single* schoolteacher, who shouldn't be entertaining men—and especially not married men—in her home at all hours of the night. When I saw you last night, you were in your nightclothes. Are you admitting that Colt was with you when you were dressed like that?" Every word the woman spoke rose higher in volume as she realized the gravity of the situation she'd just caught Kathryn in.

"Mrs. Pembrooke. I'm not going to ask you again." Jackson looked over at Clarence Pembrooke, before taking her by the arm and gently pushing her back over beside him. "Either you keep your wife quiet, or I'll take my hankie and tie it around her mouth to keep her that way myself."

"Well, I've never..." Her words stopped as Jackson stared her down, and she finally stepped back beside her husband, crossing her arms angrily over her chest.

Kathryn wouldn't meet Colt's eyes. He wanted to go over and grab her by the arms to shake some sense into her. Why couldn't she have just listened to him? Martha Pembrooke would never have had enough evidence to get him arrested for killing Constantine, but obviously Kathryn was going to make sure of it.

And now she was going to be accused of things she hadn't done either.

"I'm Kathryn Reeves, the schoolteacher who lives on the property. Colt came along, and we were outside talking for a while before we smelled the smoke." She briefly glanced his way, and he knew she was thinking about the moment they'd first noticed the smoke in the air. Thankfully, she hadn't revealed that part of the story or what they'd been doing.

"So, you can verify that Colt would have been with you in the time before the fire broke out?"

She nodded. "Yes, he was with me."

Mrs. Pembrooke gasped loudly. "Well, young lady, you can be sure your teaching career is over. I'll make sure of that."

This time, Jackson wasn't as gentle as he took her arm and led her to her buggy, almost pushing her up into the seat. "Clarence, take your wife home before I arrest her for being a nuisance."

If not for the severity of the situation, Colt wouldn't have been able to hold back his laughter when Mrs. Pembrooke sputtered, trying to speak as the buggy finally pulled away. Even as they drove down the lane toward the road, they could hear her voice hollering at her husband to take her back. Colt cringed knowing the ear-lashing the poor man was going to endure on the way home.

Jackson faced them again and shook his head. Through all of it, Caleb had stood back quietly, and now he walked forward to stand next to them. "I'd say it's just a matter of time before all of Promise hears about this, so I'm going to head back into town and try to stop things from getting too far."

"Miss, thanks for your honesty. And, Colt, I never did believe you'd done it, I hope you know that."

Colt was still watching Kathryn, who stood perfectly straight, not looking any of them in the eye. He knew she was embarrassed, and he wished he could fix all of this to save her reputation somehow.

But the damage was done, and no matter what he said now, he knew Kathryn was never going to be able to stay, even if she wanted to.

CHAPTER 22

"Oh, Kathryn. I wish you would stay at least until the community board members have a chance to meet with the superintendent of the district. I'm sure everything will be sorted out in your favor. Caleb and Fae certainly will be on your side, and I know they don't want you to leave."

Kathryn smiled sadly at her dear aunt. She'd packed up her few belongings in the cabin earlier and had come to spend her last night in Promise at the boardinghouse so she could catch the stage tomorrow.

After her announcement yesterday, it hadn't taken long for Mrs. Pembrooke to share the information with the entire town. Even though Kathryn knew most of the people who lived here were kind and forgiving, she didn't want to put them in the position of having the scandal of a teacher who had done something improper.

So she'd announced she would leave and let them find another teacher who could take over.

It had been hard to tell Delia and Owen, and Mrs. Hammond too. She'd let them know about her decision yesterday after everyone had left. Colt was gone, and she hadn't seen him since. She figured he was glad she'd made everything easier by just leaving. Although she admitted she was a bit hurt that he hadn't come down to talk to her at all, or even say goodbye, but she knew it was likely for the best.

In her heart, she knew she'd fallen in love with him, and knowing that, there was never going to be an easy way to say goodbye.

She'd told all of the children in her class this morning she was going home and let them know how much she would miss them all. It had been so hard to give them all one last hug. While some of the girls cried openly, she could tell there were even a few boys who were struggling to keep their tears back.

They didn't know the details of why she was

leaving, and she hoped even as they got older and learned the truth, they wouldn't judge her too harshly.

She'd been avoiding Fae and anyone else she knew would try convincing her to stay until the superintendent arrived to discuss the situation tomorrow. She just couldn't face the humiliation of everyone talking about her, while she waited to hear her fate. Even though she knew she hadn't really done anything inappropriate, and she was sure a lot of her friends in town knew it, having all of her transgressions discussed in a room full of people wasn't something she wanted to deal with.

So she would leave and make it easier for everyone.

It irked her that Mrs. Pembrooke would see this as a victory, but Kathryn hoped the community would be able to find another teacher who could come out here and take over so the school could keep operating. The children shouldn't have to suffer for what happened.

"It's for the best, Aunt Lucy. They can find a new teacher, and in a few months, everything will be forgotten. I could never live with myself if Delia or Owen ever heard anything bad about their father due to gossip in town. This is his home, so if I go, people will forget in time."

"But you didn't even do anything, and we all know it."

"I know, Aunt Lucy, but it's just the way of the world. Besides, I can get a good job back in Boston and will make a lot more money than I ever could out here."

Her aunt clucked her tongue and shook her head. "Kathryn Reeves, I wasn't born yesterday. We both know money has never been the reason for what you're doing. You love teaching, and you also love being out here in the country. This is where you belong."

Kathryn was too tired to argue anymore, so she turned back to look out the window at the darkening street outside. Promise had only a few gas lanterns lighting up the streets at night, and she knew Old Tom would be going around soon to light them. But right now, the street was empty from the usual bustle of wagons and people throughout the day.

She could see a light on across the street at the mercantile, and she wished she could go over to visit her friend, but she knew it would only make leaving harder.

She was going to miss the quiet life she'd started to get used to. The fresh summer air, so unlike what she'd lived with growing up, was something she would miss the most. In the city, the smell of horse manure, sweaty bodies, and smoke left her longing for air she could breathe deeply of without ever needing to carry a kerchief to cover her nose from the stench.

As she watched, a wagon hurried into town and stopped in front of the mercantile. Her eyebrows pulled together, and she stood up, immediately recognizing the figures quickly jumping down.

"Is that Winnie, and little Delia?" Her aunt had come over to see what she was looking at.

"It is. Colt must still not be home, but where's Owen? And why are they coming into town so late?"

Something in her stomach just wasn't sitting right. The way Mrs. Hammond had driven the wagon into town and then jumped out as though she was a spry child, and not an aging widow, told Kathryn something was wrong.

She hurried out the door, lifting her skirt as she ran across the street to the mercantile. As she raced up the steps, she almost collided with Caleb as he threw the door open and ran out.

"What's going on? Is Colt all right? Owen?" Kathryn gasped out.

Caleb kept going, stopping just long enough to look at her seriously and shake his head. "Owen's gone missing. He left a note and said he was leaving. Go on inside. Fae is with Mrs. Hammond and Delia. I'm going to gather some men and head out to find him."

Kathryn ran inside, with her aunt right behind her. As soon as she got through the door, Delia ran over and threw her arms around her waist.

"Miss Reeves, Owen ran away, and Pa's not home, and we don't even know where he is. Everyone is leaving me!"

Kathryn pulled the small arms from around her and crouched down, holding both of Delia's hands firmly in her own as she looked into her eyes and smiled. "Delia, don't worry. I know Mr. Bailey and all the men in this town won't stop looking for your brother until they've found him. And I'm sure your pa will be home soon too."

Tears streamed down the girl's face from red-rimmed eyes. She sniffed and shook her head. "You're leaving too."

The little voice sounded so grief-stricken, that

every single word she spoke tore at Kathryn's heart.

"Oh, sweetheart." What could she possibly say to comfort her about her own leaving? She couldn't lie and say she would stay. So, she just pulled her into her arms and let the girl sob into her shoulder. This child had already lost so much when her mother left, and now she believed everyone else she cared about was leaving too.

When they got Delia calmed down, Kathryn held her hand and led her back into Fae and Caleb's living quarters, pulling the child up to snuggle in beside her on the settee.

"He left a note saying he was going to the train. His spelling isn't that good, but at least that's what it looked like." Mrs. Hammond sat down beside them and reached out to caress Delia's hair, as she patted at her own eyes with her hankie.

"Where is Colt?" Kathryn was suddenly feeling an irrational anger toward the man who should be here looking after his own son.

Mrs. Hammond shook her head. "I don't know. After all the hubbub yesterday, he said he had to get away from here, and he was heading to Brookings so he wouldn't be back for a few days. I just never thought Owen would run away. I should have been paying more attention, but I've just been so upset about everything and I guess…"

Kathryn reached out and put her hand on the older woman's. "No, Mrs. Hammond, don't blame yourself."

Fae came over and crouched down in front of the woman. "And don't worry. I know Caleb, and he won't rest until he's found Owen. There are enough men in town who can spread out and cover a lot of ground. The boy is on foot, so he can't have gotten very far."

As the sun set completely over the horizon on the other side of town, the women couldn't do anything but sit there and pray they were right.

"We've still got men out looking, Mrs. Hammond. I just came back to let you all know what we've found so far, which isn't much. And to see if there's anything else in the note that might give us more of a hint."

Kathryn kept her arms around Mrs. Hammond's shoulders as the older woman desperately tried to think. "I should have brought it with me. I was just so upset, and I wasn't thinking clearly. If you want to ride out to the farm, Caleb, it will still be on the table where I dropped it." She shook her head sadly. "But it only had a few words, saying he was leaving home, and was headed to the train."

Caleb thrust his hands through his hair like he was trying to think. The men had been out all night looking, and he'd just come back to the mercantile as the sun was starting to peek over the buildings in town. He looked ragged, and Fae was fussing and trying to get him to sit down and have some coffee.

"We've been all spread out along the roads that would lead to the closest train station, but that's all the way in Brookings. There's no way a boy would make it that far on foot. And we're all on horseback, so unless he hitched a ride, he can't be that far."

Thankfully, Delia had fallen asleep and was tucked into a bed upstairs. The poor little girl had cried non-stop last night, sure that now she'd lost everyone in her family.

If Colt were here, Kathryn would give him a good piece of her mind for taking off and leaving the kids like this, and now not being here when his family needed him.

It was bad enough he didn't care enough to be here and say goodbye to her, but to be off doing who knows what, when his family was going through such a crisis was simply irresponsible.

Kathryn shook her head and took a deep breath. She knew she wasn't really being fair, because she knew the kind of man Colt was, and if he was aware of what was happening back here, he'd be heartbroken. If they couldn't find Owen in time, he'd probably never forgive himself. He already carried so much guilt for what happened with his wife, and how it affected his children.

Suddenly, her heart dropped to her knees. Her mind flew back to that day when Owen had gotten into a fight because he was being teased about his mother.

"Did anyone actually just look around the farm? Or, have they all followed the roads leading to Brookings?"

She was already standing up, heading to the door.

Caleb shook his head. "We started at the farm and called out to him a few times before making our way in the direction he'd be headed. Why?"

"I think I might know where he is. Caleb, can you take me out to the farm, please?"

When Kathryn caught Mrs. Hammond's hopeful gaze before she stepped out the door, she knew it would break her heart if Owen wasn't there and she'd gotten his grandmother's hopes up for nothing.

But something in her own heart told her the boy was exactly where she believed he was.

CHAPTER 23

"*J*ust wait here, Caleb. I need to crawl back into the trees a bit, but if he's in there, I think it's better if only one of us goes in."

Caleb reached up and helped her down from the wagon. "I sure hope you're right, and that he's been here the whole time. I'll just wait here by the wagon but call out if you need me. I'm sure he'll be fine, even if this is where he spent the night, but just in case..." his words trailed off as they both tried not to think the worst.

They'd parked back a bit from the little trail she knew went into the spot in the trees, because a wagon couldn't make it in this far. As she walked, she vaguely noticed the joyful songs the birds were singing around her as they welcomed the sun. This was the familiar sound she'd grown so used to every morning since moving out here, and her heart ached knowing this would be the last time she'd hear it.

She got down and started crawling into the small opening she could see, pushing branches back to make her way. When she got in a bit farther, a small sob escaped as she recognized the familiar body curled up and sound asleep on the ground.

"Owen!"

Her skirt got caught under her knees as she tried to get to him faster so she could take him in her arms. He slowly opened his eyes and looked at her, trying to make sense of where he was and what she was doing here.

Finally, the memory of why he was hiding in the trees must have come back and his eyes opened wide. "Miss Reeves! How did you find me?"

By now, she was close to him and pulled him over into her embrace. "Owen, you shouldn't have run off like that. What were you thinking?"

She could feel his small body trembling slightly,

and she realized he was likely chilled from sleeping outside all night. Even though it was the height of summer and the days were hot, the nights could often be chilly, especially for a child without enough clothes on.

She pulled her shawl from her shoulders and wrapped it around him.

"I was going to try to get to the train. But I didn't know how. So I just needed to sleep and think on things."

"You've had your poor grandmother, and Delia, and everyone else in town worried sick. And your pa isn't going to be too happy when he gets home and hears what you did." She didn't mean to scold him, but the fear of the past few hours had taken a toll on her.

She was tired. This was the second time in just a few days she'd been up all night, and the distress of everything had finally caught up to her.

But when he lifted his eyes to hers, and she watched the lone tear make its way down his cheek, she couldn't stay mad.

"What about you, Miss Reeves? Were you worried sick?"

She squinted in shock. "Owen, how could you

even ask me that? Of course I was worried. I've been up all night fretting about you."

He looked down and swallowed.

"Well, why would you be worried about me?"

Her mouth hung open, and she wasn't sure what to say. The morning songs being sung in the trees around her seemed suddenly out of place in this moment as she struggled to figure out what had made Owen run away.

"I was worried because I care about you, Owen. Surely you know that. We all care about you."

He looked up once more and held her eyes. "Then why are you leaving me too?"

All the air left her lungs as she heard the simple sentence spoken so quietly.

Owen thought she was leaving him. He didn't know what had really happened, so in his eyes, she was no better than his mother who'd walked out and left him behind.

In that moment, as she pulled him into her arms and let him cry into her shoulder, she knew she had to fix this. She couldn't just leave him too.

At least, not without a fight.

SHE STOOD PERFECTLY straight in the small church, facing the front where the superintendent of the district sat at a desk they'd set out for him to use.

Fae had tried to convince her to sit beside her on one of the pews, but Kathryn was determined to stand tall and not let them see her fear. Where just a few hours ago, she'd been prepared to leave Promise behind and go home without even arguing her case, now she was determined to win. And, if she didn't, Owen would at least be able to understand some day that she had tried to stay.

After finding him this morning, Caleb had gone back to town to get Mrs. Hammond and Delia, while Kathryn had taken Owen up to the house. After everything was settled, she'd come back to get ready for the meeting that had been arranged with the school board and superintendent.

The laws around here were a bit primitive compared to back east, but the superintendent reported to the state, and made sure the little bit of money provided to the public schools was being used wisely.

And that included having a teacher who was following the guidelines that were set out.

Looking at the tiny man hunched over the

papers in front of him, Kathryn wasn't too sure what to think of him. So far, he hadn't said much after coming inside, and just sat there reading.

Finally, he took a deep breath and looked up at her over the round glasses that sat down on the bridge of his nose. "It says here you were caught in a compromising position. Is this true?"

She held her head high as she spoke. "I wasn't caught in a compromising position, but I did admit to having a visitor who it might seem to be inappropriate."

Her cheeks started to burn as she felt all eyes on her. She knew Fae and Caleb were right behind her, along with Doc Jacobs, Reverend Moore, and a couple of other community members who made up the volunteer board.

But she also knew Mrs. Pembrooke and her husband were here, along with some of the parents from the private school who had always believed their children were more "privileged." Obviously, the Pembrookes wanted to make sure they had people on their side too.

Mrs. Pembrooke stepped forward and looked at her accusingly. "She's admitted to being with a married man, past dark, wearing only her nightgown. I don't know what is considered proper lady-like behavior in the cities back east, but out here, we don't stand for single women coming into town and throwing themselves at our menfolk."

If not for the severity of the situation, Kathryn would have burst out laughing. Did she honestly believe any single woman would be coming along and throwing themselves at her meek husband?

"And what do the board members believe we should do in this situation?" The superintendent looked over his glasses at the others in the room. "We need to think of what's best for the children and not base our decisions on any personal friendships we might have with Miss Reeves."

Her heart started to pound in her chest as she waited.

Caleb was the first to speak behind her. "As the founding member of this school board, and one who has invested a great deal of money in the school itself, including contributing money toward the wages for Miss Reeves, I intend to make my voice heard. I've known her long enough to know that if she says the situation she was in was innocent, then I believe her. And I also believe her staying as the teacher is in the best interest of the children of Promise."

The superintendent nodded and wrote something on the paper in front of him. "Anyone else have anything to say?"

"Yes, I'm about to have a child, and I believe I should have a say in who will be teaching them. Miss Reeves is the only teacher I would trust with my child."

Kathryn spun around at the sound of Mercy's voice as she came in the door. Behind her, lined up outside to come in, were faces she recognized as parents of the children in her school. All of them were holding the hands of her students who smiled when they saw her standing there.

Tears streamed down her face as one after another insisted she was the best teacher for the job, and if she wasn't here, the school may as well close down.

This made Mrs. Pembrooke excited as she nodded enthusiastically. "Yes, I'm glad everyone is finally seeing reason. There is no need for two schools in this town. If parents aren't willing to pay the fees to ensure their children get the best possible education, then it's too bad for them. But having a simple, little country schoolhouse is completely unnecessary when you have the best school in the state right on your doorstep."

"You're wrong, Mrs. Pembrooke. My little Hazel has learned more in just a few weeks at that little country schoolhouse then she'd ever learned in the months she was enrolled in your school."

Mrs. Pembrooke looked around at the now almost completely full church and shook her head in disbelief. "I can't believe every one of you is standing here condoning the behavior of your schoolteacher. Have you all forgotten that she was in a compromising position with a married man?"

Kathryn clenched her eyes closed for a moment, hoping the older children wouldn't understand what Mrs. Pembrooke was trying to say.

"Well, I'd like it to go on the record to say the only thing Miss Reeves was caught in was a situation beyond her control when I showed up at her door. She was merely outside, enjoying the evening before I arrived, and had I been a proper gentleman, I would have left."

Her eyes flew open at the sound of Colt's voice. Her throat closed and her heart pounded as he held her eyes in his gaze while walking up the middle aisle toward her. Delia and Owen were on either side, and Mrs. Hammond right behind him.

"And, I'd also like it to go on the record that she

wasn't with a married man. Not anymore." He held up some papers in his hand. "It was taking a bit longer than I'd liked for them to be signed and sent back to me by all the lawyers, so I went and got them myself." He set them down on the desk in front of the confused superintendent.

"And, you are?"

"I'm Colt Hammond, the man who Miss Reeves is accused of being in a compromising position with. And I'm here to make it right so there is no room for gossip. I'm going to marry Kathryn Reeves, and if anyone ever dares to suggest anything improper about what she did, they will answer to me."

Kathryn's mouth fell open, and she pulled her eyebrows together. She was sure she looked just as confused as the poor superintendent behind her.

"But, I'm not...shouldn't we..."

She was stammering and she didn't know what to say. His eyes had never left hers, and her mouth was suddenly dry.

"Kathryn, I'm sorry you got dragged into this when there was never anything improper about two people who cared about each other having a conversation."

"But, I don't want you to feel like you have to

marry me just to protect my name. That's not fair to you. I know you never want to marry again."

He came closer, taking her hands in his. For a moment, she forgot everyone else was in the room, breathlessly listening to every word.

"I'm not just marrying you to protect your name. I'm marrying you to protect my heart. Because I can't imagine my life without you in it. There is only one woman in the whole world who would ever make me want to marry again, and that woman is you."

Her lips opened, and she had to swallow against the lump in her throat. "But, what about the children?"

He looked down at the smiling faces looking up at them. "Well, I've talked things over with them, and they've already agreed that even if you don't want to stay here as their teacher, they would really like it if you'd stay and be their ma."

Her chin quivered as she fought against the tears. Colt reached his hand out and gently cupped her chin. "I love you, Kathryn Reeves. And if you ever thought for a moment I was going to just sit back and watch you leave, then I question your sanity."

Caleb was the first to give a happy cheer as he came over and slapped Colt on the back. "Congratulations, Colt."

But Colt's gaze was still on hers. "She hasn't agreed to anything yet, Caleb." He swallowed, and for a moment she couldn't breathe as she held his gaze. "Kathryn?"

As she looked into the eyes that were so full of hope, and what she thought was maybe a little bit of fear at her saying no and walking away, her heart burst with pure joy.

This man was her future, and even if she was never able to teach another day in her little schoolhouse, she knew she would be happy as long as she was with him.

"Yes, Colt. I will marry you."

As the cheers broke out in the church, with all the people who had become so dear to her, even Mrs. Pembrooke's high-pitched voice still arguing her case was drowned out.

She didn't even care that she was now being lifted into the arms of the man she was going to marry, in the middle of a church, and his lips were on hers in front of the entire community.

When he pulled his head back and smiled down

at her, she knew every prayer she'd ever sent up had just been answered.

She loved Colt and now she knew with certainty, he loved her too.

She was where she had always been meant to be.

EPILOGUE

"Well, my dear, I never thought it would be possible to agree with you, but I think I finally believe you made the right decision to move out here. I don't remember a time when I've seen you more happy or glowing than you are right now."

Kathryn smiled up at her father as they stood in the shade of the tree. It had been a perfect day for her wedding, and she was so happy that her family had come all the way here for it.

"Thank you for coming." She turned and grinned at her sister, Emma. "Maybe you'll want to stay out here for a while and see just how perfect life in the country really is."

Emma shook her perfectly coiffed blonde head

and laughed. "I don't know if country folk would be able to handle me."

"Well, if you ever want to come and stay here, you're always welcome. I think you'd be surprised how peaceful life can be away from the bustle of the city."

She stood back and watched as her family went over to talk to Mrs. Hammond. Since they'd arrived in town, Kathryn had been excited to see how welcoming everyone had been to them. She knew it had helped her father to understand why she loved it here.

"So, Mrs. Hammond. I know the wedding wasn't quite as fancy as the ones you would have attended back home, but I hope today was everything you could have dreamed."

Kathryn smiled warmly at her new husband as he came over and put his arm around her shoulders. She leaned her head into him and sighed deeply. "It was more than I could have dreamed of. Although I would have been happy with anything, as long as it was you I was marrying."

"Well, I knew it was probably safest to keep everything far away from open water, or require you to step out of a wagon while wearing a fancy dress, so having it here in the yard was a good idea."

She gasped and lifted her head to pretend to glare at him while she slapped his arm gently. "Colt! Why do you always have to bring up my more embarrassing moments?"

He laughed and pulled her close. "I'm sorry. But I guess it's because those moments are what made me fall in love with you. The day you fell out of my wagon, I'm pretty sure you already had my heart. And the fact that no matter how much you might have struggled, you never stopped trying to learn how to adapt to life out here."

She rolled her eyes as she remembered that day. "Maybe if you'd been more of a gentleman, I might have fallen for you then too. You're lucky I'm such a forgiving woman."

He turned her in his arms to face him. "Oh, I have no doubt about how lucky I am. I believed I had nothing to offer a woman, and that I'd never find anyone who could love me the way you do. But you fell into my life and turned everything upside down. I know I will never be able to give you the fancier things in life, but I hope you know I will always be by your side and will love you with everything I have."

She brought her hand up to his cheek. "I don't need any of the fancy things. All I need is you."

His head lowered, and their lips met. He pulled her close in his embrace as he kissed her slowly, leaving her breathless. The world around her stopped moving and for a moment, it was only them.

"Pa, hurry up! Mr. Bailey is setting up a three-legged race, and we have to win this time!"

Owen's voice interrupted them, and it took a moment for Kathryn to remember where she was. Colt still held her close, smiling down at her while he waited for her to regain her balance.

"Only a small, country wedding would have a three-legged race."

Kathryn laughed, then pulled out of his arms to take a look around her at the people who were all gathered to celebrate their wedding.

She was sure the entire community of Promise, and surrounding farms, had showed up today. Well, except for Martha and Clarence Pembrooke, who were still fuming over the fact they hadn't managed to make Kathryn lose her teaching job.

Even now, after marrying, she'd been told by the school board she could continue teaching as long as she wanted. Normally, rules for teachers were quite strict and married women could no longer teach. Kathryn had told them that she would stay on as long as she could, until she began having babies of her own.

Her new mother-in-law was happy to move down to the cabin, and Colt was already working on fixing it up to be better suited for the older woman to have her own place with better amenities.

"Well, that's not fair, Owen. I don't have a partner." Delia had followed her brother and she was standing there pouting because she wouldn't be able to join the race.

Kathryn laughed and shook her head. "Why not? Can't I be your partner again?"

Delia's mouth dropped open and she shook her head. "No, your dress might get ruined."

Kathryn looked down at the simple white dress Mrs. Hammond had sewn for her out of material from her own wedding dress. It wasn't made out of silk, but it was beautiful.

She also knew it was made out of a sturdy fabric that could withstand a little three-legged race.

"I think we'll be fine. Besides, I've been practicing."

Colt's eyebrow lifted as he stared at her. "You know, I'm not going to let you win just because you're my wife."

She shrugged and took Delia's hand to lead her over to the starting line where Caleb was gathering the racers together.

"That's good, because I don't intend to let you win just because you're my husband."

As she walked away, the sound of Colt's laughter filled her heart. And when she heard the excited chatter of these children who were now her own, she knew this little place in the middle of the prairies had given her everything she'd ever wanted.

A home, a family, and the promise of love.

I HOPE YOU ENJOYED READING, LOVE IS PATIENT. If you could take a couple minutes and head back to Amazon to leave a review, it would be greatly appreciated :)

Keep reading for some interesting notes from the book in the Afterword!

IF YOU WOULD LIKE to be notified of the release of Book 2, make sure you're signed up below…

**Newsletter SignUp:

https://www.kaypdawson.com/newsletter

**Fan Group:

https://www.facebook.com/ groups/kaypdawsonfans/

AFTERWORD

In the 1800's, divorce was not as common as it is today, and it wasn't easy to obtain. During the research for this book, I came across some interesting information about what were known as "divorce colonies".

After Mexico became a destination where wealthy couples could travel to easily get a divorce, some US states realized the potential for making money, while saving people the expense of needing to travel to Mexico.

The Dakota Territory was considered a divorce colony, where couples could get a divorce, however they had to move and become citizens of the state for a minimum period of three months.

Many couples would move for the required time, get their divorce and then leave.

In the case of Colt and his wife, it made it much easier for him to obtain his divorce from Arlene, and give him his chance for a happy ever after.

*There is a lot more information at a website I found, if you'd like to read more about the divorce colonies…

https://historycollection.com/the-american-divorce-colonies-of-the-1800s/

CHARLES INGALLS

I've always been a Little House on the Prairie fan, and the entire premise for this book came to me during a lifelong dream I'd had to visit some Laura Ingalls sites. I was staying at the homestead in De Smet, sleeping in a covered wagon on the property, when the concept for this series was born.

As I sat at a table looking across the fields at the little schoolhouse on the property and imagined life as it had been, I knew where my series needed to take place.

And, I knew I had to have a mention of the man Laura had wrote so lovingly about in her own stories.

So, while Promise is a fictional town, set nearby where real-life De Smet is, I would like to imagine Charles Ingalls might have visited the community from time to time.

Go to my Book Listing page under "My Books" on my website for all of my books, and latest releases!

KayPDawson.com

USA Today Bestselling Author, Kay P. Dawson writes sweet western romance - the kind that leaves out all of the juicy details and immerses you in a true, heartfelt love story. Growing up pretending she was Laura Ingalls, she's always had a love for the old west and pioneer times. She believes in true love, and finding your happy ever after.

Happily married mom of two girls, Kay has always taught her children to follow their dreams. And, after a breast cancer diagnosis at the age of 39, she realized it was time to take her own advice. She had always wanted to write a book, and she decided that the someday she was waiting for was now.

She writes western historical, contemporary and time travel romance that all transport the reader to a time or place where true love always finds a way.

You can connect with Kay through her website at **KayPDawson.com**

She also has an active fan group where she hangs out with her readers...https://www.facebook.com/groups/kaypdawsonfans/

Newsletter SignUp:

https://www.kaypdawson.com/newsletter

Bookbub Follow:

https://www.bookbub.com/authors/kay-p-dawson

kaypdawsonwrites@gmail.com

Made in the USA
Coppell, TX
27 April 2025

48704267R00135